LOU LOU & PEA

AND THE BICENTENNIAL BONANZA

Written by
JILL DIAMOND

Illustrated by
LESLEY VAMOS

Farrar Straus Giroux
New York

Farrar Straus Giroux Books for Young Readers
An imprint of Macmillan Publishing Group, LLC
175 Fifth Avenue, New York, NY 10010

Text copyright © 2018 by Jill Diamond
Illustrations copyright © 2018 by Lesley Frances Vamos
All rights reserved.
Printed in the United States of America by
LSC Communications, Harrisonburg, Virginia
Designed by Christina Dacanay
First edition, 2018
10 9 8 7 6 5 4 3 2 1

mackids.com

Most of the fashion quotes that Pea shares throughout the book
were borrowed from these two sources:
Patrick Mauriès and Jean-Christophe Napias, *Fashion Quotes: Stylish Wit and
Catwalk Wisdom*, New York: Thames & Hudson, 2016.
Christian Dior, *The Little Dictionary of Fashion: A Guide to Dress Sense for Every
Woman*, New York: Abrams, 2007.
The quote on page 36 is from Rachel Dixon, "Coco Before Chanel: 'She was
claiming freedom through her designs,'" *The Guardian*, July 31, 2009,
theguardian.com/lifeandstyle/2009/jul/31/coco-before-chanel.
The quote on page 187 is from Marc Jacobs, Twitter, June 19, 2014,
twitter.com/marcjacobs/status/479775731925663744.

ISBN: 978-0-374-30298-6
Library of Congress Control Number: 2017944537

Our books may be purchased for promotional, educational, or
business use. Please contact your local bookseller or the Macmillan Corporate
and Premium Sales Department at (800) 221-7945 ext. 5442 or by e-mail at
MacmillanSpecialMarkets@macmillan.com.

The activities in this book should be performed with common sense and care,
and with adult supervision. Neither the publisher nor the author assumes any
responsibility for any personal injuries or property damage resulting from the
conduct of any of the activities, or portions thereof, contained herein.

Special thanks to our Spanish language proofreader for her careful review of the text.

For Dad, who supports me no matter what I do, but who always secretly wanted me to be a writer

                                    —J.D.

To my crazy talented family for setting the achievement bar way high, and to Chris, my cheerleader, and to Lady Penelope for keeping me company

                                    —L.V.

CHAPTER ONE
PSPP

It was 3:37 p.m. and Lou Lou Bombay was where she belonged—sitting in the sunshine in her backyard garden. She wriggled her toes in the grass and smiled at a honeysuckle bush nestled between the fence and her tulips. Lou Lou glanced at a red envelope resting on the lawn next to her, and then gazed up at the clouds. One looked like a saguaro cactus, another was a wispy fern, and a third, a misshapen forget-me-not.

Lou Lou heard a knock on the backyard gate and ran to answer it.

"Greetings, Miss Lou Lou Bombay," said the small

brown-haired girl wearing a crisp school uniform. Lou Lou shielded her eyes from the sun and grinned at her best friend.

"Yay! You're finally here, Pea!" Lou Lou caught herself. "I mean, I'm so delighted you could join me for a PSPP picnic, Miss Peacock Pearl!" Lou Lou used the extra-polite tone reserved for Friday PSPP, or Post-School-Pre-Parents, a magical time when school was over for the week but Lou Lou's parents had yet to come home from work.

"I am similarly tickled, Miss Lou Lou Bombay," Pea replied.

"Would you care for PSPP tea and scones?" Lou Lou walked over to a picnic basket resting on the grass and plopped down beside it.

"Certainly, my dear," said Pea. She took a blue-and-white-checkered blanket from her schoolbag and spread it out next to Lou Lou. Pea wasn't fond of sitting on the ground, as it meant the possibility of getting dirty. As a horticulturist, Lou Lou didn't mind one bit.

While Pea got settled, Lou Lou poured tea from a thermos into mismatched teacups and opened a tin of freshly baked currant scones. She handed Pea the blue cup, of course, all the while eyeing the envelope. It was sealed with a fancy gold sticker embossed with two fancy

*B*s. Lou Lou already knew what was inside and was dying to open it. But she tried her best to keep to the PSPP tradition of polite conversation, which was not easy for her.

"How was your day at school, Miss Pearl?"

Pea smiled at Lou Lou's proper PSPP question.

"It was lovely, gracias," Pea replied. She daintily took a scone from the tin. Pea handed the tin to Lou Lou, who rooted around among the remaining scones until she found the one with the most currants. "We went on a field trip to Campo Bonito to do some painting outside of the city," Pea added, and Lou Lou nodded with a mouth full of scone.

"I trust school was pleasant for you," Pea said, and sipped her tea. Before Lou Lou could respond with a *Quite pleasant indeed, thank you*, Pea noticed the envelope and said, "Is that what I think it is?"

"Yes, it was in my mailbox when I got home!" Lou Lou replied, forgetting in her excitement that her mouth was still full.

Pea was excited, too, so she didn't seem to mind. "Let's open it!" she said.

Lou Lou exhaled deeply. She was grateful that Pea had abandoned the formalities of PSPP. "Oh, yay! I was going to burst if I had to wait one second longer!" She put down her cup, tore through the envelope's seal, and pulled out the paper inside. Pea clenched the handle of her own cup in anticipation. Lou Lou unfolded the paper and Pea peered over Lou Lou's shoulder to read the gold writing.

OFFICIAL PROGRAM FOR THE ONE,
~ THE ONLY ~
BICENTENNIAL BONANZA

Date: This Tuesday
Neighborhood Host: El Corazón
Location: Limonero Park

SCHEDULE;

10:30 AM CARACOLES CONTEST!
4:00 PM CELEBRATION & PERFORMANCES
6:00 PM GAZEBO UNVEILING

CREDITS;

BANNERS: Sarah's Studio
CANDLES: Rosa the Candle Lady
HATS: Mr Vila of Marvelous Millinery & Peacock Pearl
HONEYSUCKLE: Juan of Green Thumb Nursery & Lou Lou Bombay
PERFORMANCES: Ensemble Cast from El Corazón

Viene uno, vienen todas to celebrate the
two hundredth birthday of our city

DON'T FORGET! Preview to be held
on the 2nd of May at the Heliotrope

Lou Lou put down the program and clapped her hands. A slosh of her tea spilled onto the blanket, but Pea pretended not to notice. "It's so exciting to see our names in print. It's like we're famous, Pea!"

"¡Sí!" Pea replied. "Especially since they sent the programs to everyone in the city!"

"I can't wait for the Bonanza," said Lou Lou. "It's going to be so much fun, and we're going to be even famouser once everyone sees my beautiful honeysuckle and your amazing hats!" Lou Lou knew that *famouser* wasn't a real word, but it fit, so she used it anyway.

Pea's bright blue eyes sparkled. "Can you believe it's in just *a few weeks*?"

"I guess that brings us to the next question. Hats or honeysuckle?" Lou Lou and Pea's usual PSPP dilemma was: candles or cupcakes? Should they head to Cupcake Cabana or pay Rosa the Candle Lady a visit? But with their city's two hundredth birthday celebration fast approaching, they had to choose between visiting Lou Lou's celebratory honeysuckle in the park and going to Marvelous Millinery, the hat shop where Pea was an apprentice hatter.

"Hats, if that's all right with you," said Pea.

"Hats it is!" replied Lou Lou. She sloshed out another

glug of tea from her cup, this time onto her pants. "I'm excited to see your newest creations. Besides, I'm on watering duty tomorrow, so we can visit the honeysuckle then."

"¡Bueno!" Pea ate the last bite of her scone and brushed nonexistent crumbs off her blue dress. "We can drop in on Rosa at the candle shop on the way home," she said once she'd swallowed.

It was settled. Lou Lou and Pea cleaned up the PSPP picnic, bringing everything inside the SS *Lucky Alley*, Lou Lou's nautical-themed house. Lou Lou used an anchor-shaped magnet to hang the Bonanza program on the fridge, then turned the ship's wheel that opened the fridge door to put away the butter. Pea washed and dried the dishes with dish towels embroidered with the words *SS Lucky Alley Galley*. Lou Lou called her parents to check in before she and Pea headed out into the spring afternoon.

CHAPTER TWO
Marvelous Millinery

Lou Lou and Pea didn't have far to go to Marvelous Millinery. The hat shop was just a few blocks from Lou Lou's house. It was near Sparkle 'N Clean, their local boutique and laundry, and La Fortuna Candle Emporium, known simply as "the candle shop." The friends took their time on the way, enjoying the sights and smells of their neighborhood.

"Mmm, fresh tortillas," Lou Lou said as they passed the Castillos' house and got a whiff of dinner preparations.

"Look, Lou Lou! They're working on the Bonanza mural!" Pea pointed at people with brushes and cans of paint, hard at work transforming a bus station wall into art. At one end of the mural, the artists were almost finished painting the city's founders, Diego Soto and Giles Wonderwood. Diego was an explorer from Puerta Madreselva in Mexico, a village named for its abundance of honeysuckle. He was the inspiration for the Bonanza honeysuckle and also Pea's great-great-great-great-uncle. Giles came from Barnaby-on-Pudding in England, a famous millinery town. To honor Giles, it was Bonanza tradition to make and wear hats like the ones Pea was working on now.

"I can't wait to see your hats and my honeysuckle in the mural!" Lou Lou said. After they completed the historical side, the mural artists would paint their vision of the upcoming Bonanza celebration on the other side.

One of the artists saw Lou Lou and Pea and waved.

"¡Hola, Sarah!" the girls called to the owner of the local community crafts studio as they hurried along to the hat shop.

When Lou Lou and Pea arrived at Marvelous Millinery, the milliner, Mr. Vila, was busy placing different hats on a mannequin's head in rapid succession.

"No, no. Maybe brown, brown. Yes, yes," Mr. Vila said to the mannequin. The milliner had a habit of repeating one-syllable words. It sounded a bit odd, but he wasn't mad like some hatters, just marvelous.

The mannequin's face was stuck in a permanent plastic smile, so Lou Lou couldn't help thinking he'd be happy no matter what hat he wore. But Mr. Vila finally settled on a purple cap.

"Hola, Mr. Vila," Pea said. The milliner, engrossed in his hats as usual, jumped at the sound of Pea's voice. He turned to look at her and raised his black, bushy eyebrows. Mr. Vila was tall, with a shiny bald head. He'd once told Lou Lou and Pea that he thought hair was overrated because there were so many beautiful hats to wear.

"Greetings, Peacock," said Mr. Vila, using Pea's full name. Only Pea's parents and Lou Lou were permitted to shorten Peacock to Pea. "Hello, Lou Lou," Mr. Vila added. Lou Lou knew that Mr. Vila loved to say her name since it was already a one-syllable word repeated. Unlike Pea, Lou Lou insisted that no one call her by her full name, Louise.

"Hi, Mr. Vila," said Lou Lou. She remembered it was still PSPP, so she asked politely, "How are you today?"

"Very well well, thank you," replied the milliner. "Particularly now that I'm finished with this bowler." Mr. Vila held up a tweed hat with a rounded top.

"Looks lovely! I brought some finishing touches for my swinger hat." Pea showed Mr. Vila two ribbon rosettes.

Mr. Vila nodded. "I must say, Lou Lou, your friend is quite talented at making hats hats. I am lucky to have such a hardworking apprentice to help me prepare for the Bicentennial Bonanza." The milliner absentmindedly plucked the purple cap from the mannequin's head and put it on his own.

"You're too kind, Mr. Vila," Pea said modestly.

"And how is your honeysuckle going, Lou Lou? Or should I say 'growing'?" Mr. Vila chuckled at his own joke.

"Positively perfectly!" Lou Lou replied, not bothering with modesty. "We've planted different varieties from around the world along one side of Limonero Park. It's been a lot of work growing the honeysuckle from seed in the greenhouse, moving the plants to the park, and all of the regular pruning and watering, but it's going to look muy bonita, if I do say so myself!" Lou Lou glanced at Pea out of the corner of her eye to check her Spanish. Pea's heritage was half Mexican and she was fluent in Spanish, unlike Lou Lou, who was still learning. Pea smiled and nodded.

"Fantastic!" Mr. Vila clapped his hands. "This is sure to be the best best Bonanza ever!"

"What were past Bonanzas like, Mr. Vila?" Pea asked. The birthday Bonanza celebration for Lou Lou and Pea's city was a special event that happened every ten years. Lou Lou and Pea had been babies during the last Bonanza and didn't remember anything about it.

"Quite nice nice, but nothing like this year, I imagine. It's the Bicentennial Bonanza, after all. And a two hundredth birthday only happens once in two hundred years!"

"Plus, we're hosting!" Lou Lou added. The different neighborhoods in the city took turns hosting the Bonanza. Lou Lou and Pea's neighborhood, El Corazón, was lucky that its turn fell on the city's two hundredth birthday. "That makes it extra special."

"Very true true!" replied Mr. Vila. He touched his head and discovered the mannequin's cap. "Oh dear! I'd forgotten that I'd taken this from you." Mr. Vila returned the cap to the mannequin's head. "I'm sorry, good good fellow. How embarrassing for me."

"It's okay, Mr. Vila. As the designer Yves Saint Laurent said, 'Isn't elegance forgetting what one is wearing?'" Pea had a new book of fashion quotes, and she was excited to use them.

"Yeah, and as Fanny Flower said, 'Worms can do wonders for the soil.'" Lou Lou wanted to contribute her own horticulture quotes, but they were more difficult to find than fashion quotes, so she'd started making them up. However, her quotes often didn't quite fit the situation.

Pea and Mr. Vila both blinked at Lou Lou, but Pea quickly broke the awkward silence. "I'd better get to work!" She and Lou Lou went into the little workshop behind Marvelous Millinery's showroom. Pea retrieved her hat-in-progress and placed it on the workshop's wooden table while Lou Lou looked around. She'd been there many times before, but each time there were more hats stacked from floor to ceiling on shelves and in various cabinets. Even though the room was nearly overflowing with hats— each one a unique creation—Pea had them immaculately organized by color, size, and style. Lou Lou moved to admire the red section, bumping into a shelf on the way and nearly causing a yellow-hat avalanche.

"What do you think, Lou Lou? Should I add one ribbon rosette or two?" Pea asked, holding up the felted hat.

"Two," Lou Lou replied. "You can never have too many ribbon rosettes."

"I agree." Pea examined the hat with keen eyes and chose the best spot for the silk flowers, right above the brim on the left. She picked up her needle and thread and attached the flowers with a few stitches. Lou Lou clapped her hands.

"It's a masterpiece!" she said, pushing curls from her face and leaning closer to get a better look at the hat. "So many colors. You've really captured an impressive spectrum of roses."

"What should I name it?" asked Pea. Like boats, flower varieties, and great works of art, all of Pea's hats had names.

"Maybe something related to the flowers," Lou Lou said. "That one's clearly a Sunrise Luxury." She lightly patted the apricot-colored rosette and identified the rose variety. "And that's one of my favorite varieties, Lady Rouge." Lou Lou pointed at the red rosette that Pea had just attached.

"How about if I name it Lady Lou Lou's Luxury?" Pea suggested.

"I love it! But you don't have to name another hat after me," Lou Lou said, although she secretly hoped that Pea would ignore this advice. Pea had already named two hats for her friend. A top hat covered in pink tulle was Lou Lou's Tutu, and a head-wrap-style one made from sari material was Bombay Bazaar.

"Está bien. You're my best friend, after all. And I've made so many!" Pea gazed proudly at the hats. "Just a few more to go. I need to have enough for every person in El Corazón who is involved in the festivities. And that's a lot of heads!"

Lou Lou laughed. "Should we go to the candle shop now?" she asked.

"That sounds like a fabulous idea," Pea replied. She began carefully putting her hat-making supplies into a bin labeled with her initials. Lou Lou wandered back into the showroom and saw a petite woman with bobbed gray hair and a pretty red blouse greeting Mr. Vila.

"Abuela Josie!" Lou Lou ran to hug Pea's grandmother Josefina Flores. At the sound of her abuela's name, Pea emerged from the workshop to join in the hug.

"Hola, mijas. I was hoping I'd see you here." Abuela Josie smiled, and her brown eyes crinkled at the sides. Pea's abuela looked a lot like Pea except for the blue eyes, which Pea had inherited from her father's side of the family.

"Did you come to see my hats?" asked Pea.

"I always love looking at your newest creations! But I'm here for another reason, I'm afraid." Abuela Josie reached into her bag and took out a black suede hat with a thick silver chain around the bottom of the crown. The hat was definitely old, but it looked well cared for except for the big chunk missing from the crown. She handed the hat to Mr. Vila.

"Oh oh! My my!" said the hatter.

"What happened to it?" asked Pea.

"I left it at the city farm and stables overnight, and I suspect an animal decided it would make a good breakfast. It wasn't in perfect shape to start, but it's unwearable now. It's my lucky vaquera hat!" Abuela Josie put one hand over her eyes. "I can't perform at the Bonanza without it! No sé que voy a hacer."

In her youth, Abuela Josie had traveled to rodeos across the country as a professional stunt-riding vaquera. She was most famous for her one-foot-drag, around-the-world, belly-flip combo, a stunt that Abuela Josie would perform for the first time in twenty years at the Bonanza. She said she was too old to pull off the belly-flip part, but she'd been hard at work practicing the one-foot-drag, around-the-world combo.

"Don't worry, Abuela Josie! I'm sure Pea and Mr. Vila can fix it. Right?"

Mr. Vila coughed and Pea looked worried. Lou Lou immediately felt bad for sounding so confident.

"I'm not sure how . . ." Pea trailed off as Abuela Josie's face fell even farther.

"Your abuelo, descanse en paz, gave it to me at the start of my vaquera career. I don't think I can pull off the stunt without it." Lou Lou and Pea knew that Abuela Josie was already nervous about performing her stunt after so long. Without her lucky hat, she'd be even more so.

"It will be hard work, but I'm sure we can do it," Pea said. She was smiling, but her fists were clenched.

"Gracias, nieta. Lo sé, lo único que puede hacer es su mejor." Abuela Josie gave Pea another hug. "Now I must be off to the shoemaker before he closes. My riding boots desperately need new fringe."

"I was just about to go out for supplies, so I'll walk with you," Mr. Vila said. "We need to make at least fifteen more fedoras, ten more homburgs, perhaps nine nine cowboy hats, seven berets . . ." Mr. Vila was still listing hats and numbers as he and Abuela Josie hurried out the front door.

When they were gone, Pea turned to Lou Lou with wide blue eyes. "I don't know how to fix this." She stuck her hand through the gaping hole in the hat's crown. "The hole will be nearly impossible to patch well. I can't match the black suede since it's so faded. I'll let down Abuela Josie and she won't perform at the Bonanza!"

Lou Lou put her arm around her best friend. "Don't worry. I don't know much about hat-making, but I'll try to help. We'll figure it out together!"

"I suppose you're right," Pea said. She still sounded concerned, but at least she'd unclenched her fists.

"¡Perfecto!" said Lou Lou. "It's not a hatastrophe, Pea! Now we'd better get to the candle shop. PSPP is almost over!"

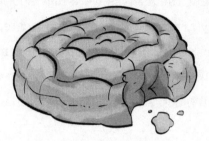

CHAPTER THREE
Candles and Caracoles

When they arrived at the candle shop, Lou Lou and Pea were greeted by Rosa's pet bunny, Helado. He bounded over, cocked his head, and gave Lou Lou a once-over with his amber eyes, then jumped directly into Pea's arms. Lou Lou didn't mind. It wasn't as if Helado didn't like her—she'd once helped rescue him from a nasty bunnynapping—but Pea had a way with animals.

"Hola, mi pequeño." Pea kissed the bunny's ears and placed him gently on the floor.

Lou Lou and Pea looked around the candle shop. It had changed a lot since Rosa had taken it over. The shop was still dim, and the tall, brightly colored candles provided most of the light, creating a sense of mysticism. But much to Pea's delight the shelves were now spotless, and Rosa had carefully arranged the candles by category.

Today, Rosa was nowhere to be seen, but her cousin Jeremy was behind the shop's counter. As usual, he was dressed in all black, so Lou Lou nearly missed him in the shadowy space.

"Buenas tardes, Jeremy," Pea called. "It's nice to see you."

"Hiya, Peacock!"

"You dyed your hair!" Lou Lou exclaimed. "When did you do that?" She'd run into Jeremy just yesterday when he was leaving his sixth-grade homeroom, and his hair had been the same as always.

Jeremy laughed at Lou Lou's outburst. "Hello to you, too, Lou Lou Bombay! And yep, I dyed it last night. I needed a change." Jeremy rolled his fingers around a piece of his bright-red spiky hair. His studded metal bracelet gleamed in the flickering candlelight. "Didn't want people thinking I was feeling blue all the time." He winked. "Whaddya guys think?"

"It looks good," Lou Lou said. Pea smiled but looked down. Lou Lou knew that she much preferred Jeremy's

blue hair—it was her favorite color, after all—but she was way too polite to tell him. When Pea looked up again, she said, "According to Christian Dior, red is 'a very energetic and beneficial color.'"

"Cool. If Mr. Dior approves, that's good enough for me," Jeremy replied.

"Where's Rosa?" asked Lou Lou.

"She had to deliver a candle to a customer," Jeremy said. "So I'm minding the shop and bunnysitting. Hey, how were my currant scones?"

"Delisho!" replied Lou Lou.

"She means *delicioso*," said Pea.

"As long as she's saying they're yummy, I'll take the compliment," said Jeremy. "Rosa and I were just discussing my baking. I'm still working on the caracoles for the Bonanza and I can't figure out el último ingrediente. You know, the one that gives it that extra kick!" To illustrate his point Jeremy kicked his foot up into the air, nearly hitting Helado's floppy ear with a black leather boot.

"Have you tried honey?" asked Lou Lou. "Or maybe agave?"

"Yes, and just about everything else I can think of," Jeremy said. "So far, no luck. They have to be ready in a few weeks for the caracoles contest!" Lou Lou nodded.

The caracoles contest was in the morning on the day of the Bonanza. The winner would receive a trophy and the honor of serving caracoles, the city's signature pastry, at the celebration later that afternoon. "My caracoles taste good, just not like the ones that Señora Basa used to make. And I want them to be killer!"

"Why would you want your caracoles to kill people?" Pea asked.

Jeremy laughed. "I meant *killer* as in *awesome* and *super-duper* and *out-of-this-world.* I brought the latest batch for Rosa to sample, if you guys feel like trying 'em out."

"Sure!" Lou Lou was full from Jeremy's PSPP scones, but she couldn't resist a nibble.

Jeremy opened a paper bag on the candle shop counter and pulled out two caracoles, handing one each to Lou Lou and Pea. "Tell me whatcha think. And be honest even if you hate them. I suppose I can take it." He sighed theatrically.

Lou Lou laughed at Jeremy's drama. "Since when have we ever *hated* anything you baked, Jeremy? I mean, it's true your blueberry muffins could use some work, but still . . ."

"There's a first time for everything," replied Jeremy. "Now enough chatting—more munching." Lou Lou turned her caracol over in her hand. It was a long length of flaky sweet dough wound into the shape of a snail. In the center of the caracol's doughy shell was a little well of custardy cream. This was Lou Lou's favorite part, and she usually licked out the cream before eating the rest. But this time, she bit straight into the dough, taking her role as a taste tester very seriously.

"It's really good," she said, forgetting to not talk with her mouth full.

"Yes," Pea agreed, dabbing her lip with her blue handkerchief.

"But . . ." Lou Lou said, just as Pea said, "Pero . . ."

". . . they don't taste like Señora Basa's caracoles." Jeremy finished their sentences.

"Right," agreed Lou Lou, thinking back to the perfect caracoles from the Panadería Basa, El Corazón's beloved Mexican bakery, which had been owned by Pea's abuela's cousin. Lou Lou and Pea had spent many happy hours at the panadería, feasting on caracoles, conchas, and tres leches cake, as well as enjoying the company of Señora Basa, who always had a good story about the old days in El Corazón or the history of Pea's family. Unfortunately, Señora Basa had passed away last year, taking the secret caracoles recipe with her.

Jeremy threw his hands in the air, startling Helado. "Woe!" he cried ridiculously, and Lou Lou couldn't help but laugh.

"Don't worry, they're still muy sabroso!" Pea could never bear the thought of hurting a friend's feelings.

"But they need to be *perfect* for the Bonanza," replied Jeremy. "I might as well just make my mediocre blueberry muffins if I can't get the caracoles recipe right."

"Well, as someone—I can't remember who—said, 'Always fertilize your peonies in the daytime,'" Lou Lou said, trying a horticulture quote. Jeremy looked puzzled.

"Maybe a candle would help," Pea said. She went to the shelf marked *Velas Artes y Transformación*. Lou Lou and Pea owned many candles from this group, including a Moda Fabulosa candle for Pea's design endeavors and a Floración candle to help Lou Lou's honeysuckle bloom. Pea held up a Gastrónomo candle with a picture of a chef on its glass holder.

"Rosa suggested that one, too. I'll try it, but it's also back to the kitchen for me," said Jeremy.

The clock on the wall struck the quarter hour. "Lou Lou, we'd better get going," Pea said. "PSPP is almost over. ¡Adiós, Jeremy!"

"Good luck with that secret-ingredient thing!" Lou

Lou called to Jeremy as she followed Pea outside. "You'll get it right!" Like Pea, Jeremy seemed to need some encouragement.

"I sure do hope so, Lou Lou Bombay!" Jeremy called back.

Outside, Lou Lou linked arms with Pea for the stroll back to the SS *Lucky Alley*. Despite today's obstacles, Lou Lou felt like the Bonanza preparations were progressing wonderfully. She and Juan were horticulture masters of the honeysuckle, Jeremy was on the road to making killer caracoles, and she was sure Pea would find a creative way to fix Abuela Josie's hat. However, come next Friday's PSPP, everything would be different in a way Lou Lou could never have predicted.

CHAPTER FOUR
Coco Chanel or Coconut

Friday night after PSPP, Lou Lou stayed over at Pea's house. Lou Lou was going to miss her mom's Saturday-morning banana pancakes and a visit with her beloved garden at first light. But she got to have a sleepover with her best friend, and that was just as good.

Lou Lou woke up to find Pea's cat Dos resting his bushy tail on her forehead. She brushed it aside before she sat up in bed. Dos meowed in protest.

Lou Lou rubbed the sleep from her hazel eyes and looked around. Sunlight streamed in through gauzy navy curtains, sending crisscrossed beams along the blue walls. Pea's room was always tidy and clean. Her books were alphabetized on the shelf, her clothes were organized by shade of blue in the closet, and every corner was dusted and spotless. Lou Lou didn't share Pea's love of cleaning, just like Pea didn't share Lou Lou's enjoyment of gardening. But the friends had many things in common, including an appreciation for each other's differences.

Lou Lou watched the clock until it struck eight, which she thought was a perfectly reasonable time to wake her best friend.

"Pea." Lou Lou tapped lightly on Pea's polka-dot-pajamaed shoulder. Uno, Pea's other cat, woke up, glared at Lou Lou, and scampered off Pea's chest. "Pea!" Lou Lou spoke louder and tapped a bit harder.

"Mmmhmph," Pea mumbled. She was definitely not a morning person. "Ese sombrero necesita más plumas antes de estar listo para la koala." Lou Lou wasn't sure what Pea had said exactly, but it was something about a hat and a koala. Lou Lou *was* sure that Pea was dreaming.

"Wake up," Lou Lou said. "We have to go to the park!" Pea finally opened her eyes.

"Good morning." Pea yawned. "I was having such a funny dream."

Lou Lou laughed. "I could tell. Let's get dressed and go!" Pea nodded and fifteen minutes later, the girls were out the door.

It was a dry April, which was good for after-school strolls and PSPP tea in Lou Lou's garden. But it also meant that Lou Lou and Juan had to regularly water the Bonanza honeysuckle.

When they reached Limonero Park, Lou Lou said, "Kyle alert!" and pointed at the ruddy-faced boy she and Pea had known forever.

Pea wrinkled her nose. "Not just Kyle alert! Kyle *and his goats* alert!"

Kyle Longfellow was standing in the center of a messy ring of five goats, waving his hands like he was conducting a goat symphony. The goats were wearing tinfoil hats decorated with wire shaped to look like stars and planets.

"No, Jupiter!" Kyle said to one of the goats as Lou Lou and Pea approached. "Don't eat your supersonic satellite helmet!" Jupiter had managed to shake off his hat and was munching on the tinfoil. "C'mon, Jupiter! Comet Cop's celestial sheep warriors would never do that!" The goat ignored Kyle's scolding and kept nibbling. Kyle always wanted to be just like his favorite comic book

superhero, Comet Cop, who had a battalion of sheep warriors to accompany him on space patrols. Kyle planned
to show off his own warriors at the Bonanza, but he
could only find goats to play the role.

Kyle noticed Lou Lou and Pea. He straightened up
and cleared his throat loudly. "Caprine troops! Fall into
line!" he commanded the goats, using his deeper Comet
Cop voice. They responded by grazing on the park grass.
Another one shook off his hat and joined Jupiter in a
tinfoil snack.

The scene reminded Lou Lou of something, and Pea
had the same thought. "Abuela Josie's hat! Lou Lou, do
you think a goat—" Pea started,
but Lou Lou was already
marching toward Kyle.

"Kyle!" Lou Lou called. "Did one of your goats eat a lucky hat?"

"What? Of course not! These are *very* responsible goats, Lou Lou Bombay! They clean up our city's parking lots and hillsides." Kyle's dad was in charge of the official city goat-landscaping program and had let Kyle borrow the goats for the Bonanza. "And now they are my special space forces. They would never eat a hat!" Lou Lou raised an eyebrow at Jupiter, who was still munching on his foil helmet.

"It was my abuela's hat," Pea explained, coming to stand next to Lou Lou. "She needs it so she can perform her stunt, and it was ruined."

"Oh. Sorry, Peacock." Kyle patted Pea's arm awkwardly. He had an obvious crush on Pea, even though Pea never wanted to acknowledge it. "But it definitely wasn't one of my space goats. Maybe a stray from a renegade battalion. As you can see, my goats are very obedient. OW!" Jupiter stepped on Kyle's foot.

"They don't appear to be paying much attention to you," Lou Lou observed.

"Don't you worry, they'll be in tip-top shape and ready for space patrol before the Bonanza. If you guys stick around, maybe I can get Mercury to do his bleat-and-retreat maneuver." Mercury butted Kyle in the leg with his head.

"No, gracias." Pea moved back a few steps. As much as Pea liked animals, she wasn't particularly fond of ones that ate garbage and were always rather dirty.

Kyle tried a different tactic. "Hey, did you guys read the book about the peacock?" He loved to make bad jokes about Pea's name. "It's a lovely tail!" Kyle delivered the punch line without waiting for an answer. "Get it? I said tail, like what a peacock has, but it also means tale, like a story."

"I got it, Kyle," Lou Lou said.

"What about you, Peacock? Did you think my joke was funny?"

Pea smiled politely. "It wasn't the worst joke I've ever heard," she said. That seemed to satisfy Kyle, who puffed out his chest and cleared his throat.

"What are you Earthling civilians doing for the rest of the day?" Kyle asked in his Comet Cop voice. "I was thinking of going on a top-secret cosmic mission. If you want, you can come along."

"We're here to water my honeysuckle, so we have to get a move on," Lou Lou said. "Please make sure your 'obedient' goats don't decide to snack on any of the plants."

"Okay, maybe another time." Kyle seemed disappointed.

"Yes," Pea politely agreed.

Kyle brightened. "Well, then, until I see you again, remember to follow the rules of the universe and never drive your spacecraft to the dark side of the moon without a permit."

·>〉•〈<·

Lou Lou and Pea headed to the far side of the rectangular park where the honeysuckle grew in a line among the lemon trees. There were twenty or more plants of different varieties, ranging from Mexican honeysuckle with its fiery orange flowers to yellow-flowered common honeysuckle with red berries. Lou Lou quickly watered the plants, and when they'd all had their daily drink, she noticed Pea gazing dreamily around the park.

"What are you looking at?" Lou Lou joined her best friend.

"I'm just imagining how the hats will look on everyone during the Bonanza."

"Fabulous, clearly," Lou Lou said. "Limonero Park is a very elegant and fashionable setting." Lou Lou knew Pea would like this.

"You're right. 'Fashion is not something that exists in dresses only. Fashion is in the sky, in the street. Fashion has to do with the ideas, the way we live, what is happening.'"

Before Lou Lou could reply, a voice behind them said, "Fashion in the sky? Ha! That's just ridiculous!" Lou Lou and Pea turned and saw a round-faced girl with long hair in braids. She was wearing a red-and-white-diamond-patterned dress and, although she was taller than Lou Lou and Pea, she looked to be a year or two younger. The girl's childish comment reminded Lou Lou of her former school nemesis, Danielle Desserts. But these days, Danielle was just snobby, and this girl had an edge to her voice that sounded downright mean. "What kind of ninny says stuff like that?" the girl asked Pea.

Pea looked shocked. "It's a quote from

Coco Chanel. One of the most famous fashion designers of all time," she replied.

"I don't care if it was Coco Chanel or coconut, it's still stupid and—"

"I'm sorry. Who *are* you?" Lou Lou interrupted. Her ears were burning and had turned a cherry color, which happened anytime she was excited or angry.

"Amanda Argyle, of course," said the girl. "Everyone knows me. Who are *you*?"

"Lou Lou Bombay and Peacock Pearl," answered Lou Lou. Pea didn't chime in with a *Pleased to meet you*, so Lou Lou knew she was definitely irritated. "Everyone in El Corazón knows us," Lou Lou added.

"Well, I don't live in El Corazón. I'm from Verde Valley," Amanda said. "And *nobody* has heard of you there."

"I doubt that's true," said Lou Lou. "You probably saw our names in the Bonanza program. My friend—who you were just very rude to—is the apprentice hatter and I'm—"

"Oh, so you're the Peacock Pearl making the Bonanza hats!" Amanda Argyle sounded interested, but her smile seemed more like a sneer.

"Did you really think there were two people with that

name?" asked Lou Lou. Amanda ignored Lou Lou's question and turned to go. "What are you doing in Limonero Park?"

Amanda turned back. "Checking out Bonanza stuff, duh. The celebration is not just for your precious little neighborhood." Lou Lou couldn't argue with this. Even though El Corazón was the official host neighborhood, the Bonanza celebrated the birthday of the whole city, so everyone was invited. "Although you all seem to think so," Amanda continued. "In fact, El Corazón thinks it's better than everyone else, what with your murals, and candle shop, and delicious cupcakes, and friendly people." Despite her harsh tone, Amanda looked wistful.

Lou Lou thought about this. She loved her neighborhood, but she'd never considered it "better" than the other places in the city. "That's not true," she said. "No one thinks that."

"It's what my daddy says, so it *must* be true," Amanda replied. "I'm leaving now. I won't say it was nice to meet you. But it was certainly interesting."

"Interesting to—to meet you, too, I suppose," Pea finally stammered, only partially recovering her politeness. Lou Lou and Pea stared as Amanda Argyle marched away, her long braids swinging behind her. Halfway across the park something fell out of Amanda's backpack.

"Hey!" Lou Lou yelled, but Amanda kept on going until she reached a car at the park's entrance. She got in and the car zipped off toward Verde Valley. Lou Lou ran over to see what Amanda had dropped. Much to her surprise, it was a honeysuckle cutting.

"Is that from one of your plants?" asked Pea when she joined Lou Lou.

Lou Lou nodded. "I wonder what she wants with it," she said. "I mean, our honeysuckle *is* beautiful, but it seems strange that she'd take a cutting."

"Maybe she's a horticulturist like you," offered Pea.

"Doubtful," replied Lou Lou. "Horticulturists are never that rude. Except that one boy who insulted someone's prize ficus and another girl who—" Lou Lou interrupted her own thought. "Actually, they can be rude. But her fingernails were too clean for her to be a horticulturist!"

"Let's just forget about her," said Pea. "She was quite unpleasant, and I'd hate for her to ruin our day."

"I don't like that she was mean to you and to El Corazón." Lou Lou wasn't as good as Pea at letting things go. "But I guess you're right. Let's stop at my house before we go to Marvelous Millinery. I bet my dad will make us iceberg burgers for lunch."

By the time they'd left the park, Lou Lou had successfully put Amanda out of her mind. After all, she and Pea had plenty of better things to think about, not the least of which was the upcoming Bonanza!

CHAPTER FIVE
A Putt-Putt-the-Puli Emergency

On the way home from Limonero Park, Lou Lou and Pea stopped to get a close-up look at the finished historical section of the Bonanza mural. El Corazón was filled with community-created murals that were greatly loved by the two friends and had even helped them solve a mystery. But today, instead of looking for clues, Pea was hoping for creative inspiration for her hat-making. Fixing Abuela Josie's lucky hat was top priority, but Pea also needed to design a few more Bonanza hats.

When they arrived at the mural, Lou Lou and Pea spent a moment in quiet contemplation. Lou Lou admired the bundle of flowered branches and vines in

Diego's arms, and Pea looked closely at Giles's jaunty cap. They both smiled at the elaborately painted gazebo that the artists had added to the background.

"Do you feel inspired?" Lou Lou asked Pea.

"The mural is definitely helping," Pea replied. "I will make a cap that looks like the one Giles is wearing."

"But it's so simple compared to your other fancy Bonanza hats," Lou Lou said.

"Yes, but as Giorgio Armani said, 'The essence of style is a simple way of saying something complex,'" Pea replied.

Lou Lou considered this. "That might be true, but the elaborate ones are way more fun!" Pea laughed, and Lou Lou looked back at the mural. "How about making a hat to represent every neighborhood in our city?" she suggested. "The one for El Corazón could be covered in hearts, the hat for Centro Circle, could have . . . well . . . circles. Verde Valley's could be green, Dove Heights could be covered with birds, and so on."

"That's a wonderful idea, Lou Lou!" said Pea. She looked at the painting of Diego's flowers. "I can't wait to add some faux-silk honeysuckle to my designs. The shipment Mr. Vila ordered should arrive today!" She clapped her hands. "Lou Lou, that's it!"

"That's what?" asked Lou Lou.

"I'll use the silk honeysuckle to cover the hole on Abuela Josie's hat! Then I won't need a perfect patch. It will just look like I added flair in honor of the Bonanza and my tío Diego!"

"Wonderful!" Lou Lou said. "You're a true hat genius!"

Pea smiled and gazed at the gazebo in the mural. "I can't wait to see what *our* gazebo will look like!" she said.

The founders of the city had been strangers to each other when they arrived, but quickly became the best of friends. To celebrate their new friendship and home, Diego and Giles built a fancy gazebo like the ones in England, but painted it with colorful flowers and designs that resembled Mexican Talavera pottery. The original gazebo had been destroyed in an earthquake, but in honor of the Bicentennial Bonanza, the city was building a replica for Limonero Park.

"I know! It's going to be amazing!" Everyone in El Corazón was very excited about the new gazebo, including Lou Lou and Pea, who planned to enjoy PSPP tea and scones under its beautiful dome.

Lou Lou linked arms with Pea. "Do you have enough inspiration?" she asked. Pea nodded. "Great, because I'm starving!"

"Let's go!" said Pea, and the two best friends headed off in the direction of the SS *Lucky Alley* for lunch.

· ›› • ‹‹ ·

Lou Lou and Pea spent Saturday afternoon and most of Sunday at Marvelous Millinery working on the Bonanza hats. Pea mended Abuela Josie's lucky hat, and under Pea's watchful blue eye, Lou Lou helped with the other Bonanza hats by sewing and gluing buttons, ribbons, silk flowers, and plastic fruits on hats of all shapes and sizes.

By the end of the weekend, they'd made excellent progress. Pea not only fixed the hole in her abuela's hat and added gorgeous sprigs of silk honeysuckle, she also cleaned the suede and polished the silver chain so it looked as good as new. At the end of the day, she held it up for Lou Lou and Mr. Vila to admire.

"Pea, that's amazing! Now Abuela Josie can do her stunt worry-free, wearing her lucky hat. She is going to be so proud of you!"

"Oh yes, yes! Fabulous work!" the milliner chimed in. Pea beamed.

·>> • <<·

That evening, Lou Lou was relaxing in the living room of the SS *Lucky Alley* with her parents. Dolphin sounds played over the speakers, making *kee kee kee* noises. Lou Lou's dad practiced sailing knots, and her mom made origami birthday cakes to use as Bonanza decorations. Lou Lou worked on a list of horticulture supplies she needed for the honeysuckle. At six o'clock, Lou Lou's dad silenced the dolphins and turned on the news.

"Good evening, folks," the newscaster said. "Tonight we will take you inside the kitchen of Cupcake Cabana for an exclusive tour. But first, an announcement from our mayor." Lou Lou looked up from her list. She was certain that Mayor Montoya was going to say something about the Bonanza. Maybe she wanted to offer a special thank-you to the girl who'd grown such beautiful honeysuckle in Limonero Park.

The news camera cut to the mayor sitting behind her desk. She was wearing a gray dress and a somber expression.

"Buenas noches, everyone," said Mayor Montoya in her smooth politician's voice. "I'm afraid I have some rather unfortunate news. I received word today that Putt Putt, my mother's puli, is very sick."

"How can a pulley get sick?" Lou Lou asked. She thought about the pulley she used to bring things up to the crow's nest, her bedroom at the tip-top of the SS *Lucky Alley.*

"It's pronounced *pool-ee.* And it's a dog," Jane Bombay, Lou Lou's mom, said. She pointed to a picture on the television of what appeared to be a black mop. Upon closer inspection, Lou Lou could just make out the mop's little pink tongue.

The camera cut back to Mayor Montoya. "I'm sorry to say that I must leave the city to visit my mother and help care for poor Putt Putt. With the Bicentennial Bonanza right around the corner, I realize this is very bad timing. But never fear, the vice-mayor will be in charge while I'm gone. He has assured me that he will take good care of the Bonanza preparations, so you will be in excellent hands. And if there is an emergency, he'll know how to contact me. I can't say exactly when I'll return, but I do hope it's in time for the celebration."

The camera cut back to the newscaster, and Lou Lou's dad turned down the television volume. "How sad. I hope Putt Putt is okay," he said.

Lou Lou squinted at her mom. "Who is the vice-mayor?" she asked. "And what does he do when there's no Putt-Putt-the-puli emergency?"

Lou Lou's mom scratched her head. "His name is Andy something," she finally replied. "I saw him driving

a little car in a parade, but honestly, I'm not sure what his regular responsibilities are." Lou Lou and her mom looked at Lou Lou's dad.

"Well, shiver me timbers, I don't know either, lassies," he said. "All I remember about him is that he wears flashy clothes."

Lou Lou thought for a moment. She was curious about the vice-mayor and sad for Putt Putt the puli. As far as the Bonanza preparations went, though, everything seemed okay. So why were her ears tingling a warning?

"I guess if the mayor says we're in good hands, it's no big deal," Lou Lou said, dismissing her ears. At the time, Lou Lou had no way of knowing it would turn out that her ears were right and she was terribly wrong.

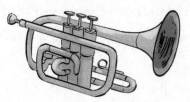

CHAPTER SIX
The Preview

The next day was a normal Monday at Lou Lou's school, El Corazón Public. There was plenty of talk of the Bonanza, and Lou Lou felt proud when she saw the red program on the hall bulletin board. Kids practiced performances for the celebration, with a spontaneous gymnastics demonstration and a trumpet concert. There was also some discussion of the mayor's sudden departure. Lou Lou asked her classmates about the vice-mayor, but, again, no one knew much about him. One kid thought he might be a friend of her uncle, and another said he once saw the vice-mayor at Cupcake Cabana.

After lunch, Lou Lou had Art. She'd been looking forward to today's class because Sarah was helping them make banners for the Bonanza.

"Go ahead and roll out the paper!" On Sarah's command, Lou Lou began to unroll a giant scroll from one end.

"Don't pull so hard on your side until I'm ready!" a high-pitched voice squealed.

"Sorry." Lou Lou slowed down and grinned at blond, petite Danielle Desserts, who was unrolling the paper opposite Lou Lou. Danielle looked away and adjusted her pink sparkly headband, but Lou Lou saw the glimmer of a smile on her face. Danielle and Lou Lou weren't exactly friends, and Danielle and her snooty-girl posse were by far the bossiest kids in the school. But she and Lou Lou had come a long way from the enemies they had once been.

When the blank scroll of paper was fully unrolled, Lou Lou's classmates drew in big block letters: ¡BIENVENIDOS A BONANZA DE BICENTENARIO! and WELCOME TO THE BICENTENNIAL BONANZA! Their handwriting was good, but not as pretty as Pea's. It was no wonder that she went to a special arts school. In smaller letters, other kids wrote the names of all the neighborhoods in the city. Then Lou Lou and her classmates added glitter and drew designs to make the banners colorful and shiny.

"Great!" Sarah said when they were finished. "Now it's time for one more banner. This one will thank our city for the lovely gift of the gazebo. Please draw pictures of how you will use the gazebo so this banner will be truly special!"

On the second banner, Lou Lou's classmates wrote: ¡GRACIAS POR EL MIRADOR! and THANK YOU FOR THE GAZEBO! Lou Lou drew herself and Pea wearing Pea's hats and enjoying PSPP tea and scones in the new gazebo. In Kyle's drawing, he stood in the gazebo in his silver Comet Cop outfit, holding his meteor blaster, which was really just streamers attached to a spatula.

"I did a good job on the galactic gazebo." Kyle admired his artwork.

"It looks great, but I don't see how the gazebo will be galactic," said Lou Lou. "It won't have rockets or orbit the sun."

"Mayor Montoya said that the gazebo will be for everyone to use however they'd like. So *I'm* using it as a space lair. Plus, everything on Earth orbits the sun, Lou Lou Bombay." Lou Lou had to admit that Comet Cop Kyle made some valid points.

In addition to Lou Lou's and Kyle's drawings, a boy sketched himself playing the accordion in the gazebo, there was a drawing of two girls eating ice cream, and another of a boy riding his neon-orange skateboard. Lou Lou squinted at Danielle's gazebo sketch of herself and her friends dressed in pink with their hips twisted to one side.

"What are you doing in this drawing, Danielle?"

"The Sugar Mountain Sisters' Shimmy. Duh!" replied Danielle.

"Oh, of course." Lou Lou was careful not to let Danielle see her giggle. Danielle and her snooty-girl posse took their obsession with Shelly and Sherry from the Sugar Mountain Sisters book series very seriously.

They would perform the sisters' dance on the afternoon of the Bonanza celebration.

Sarah took a step back to survey the two banners. "These look great!" she said. "Everyone should be proud of their work. The banners will be on display tomorrow at the Preview, and then we'll hang them at the Bonanza celebration, of course. This Bicentennial Bonanza is truly going to be an occasion to remember!"

As Lou Lou helped Sarah carefully re-roll the paper, Sarah's words, *occasion to remember*, echoed in Lou Lou's head. She was certain that the Bonanza would be one of the most memorable events of her life so far, and she could hardly wait another few weeks for the celebration!

· >> • << ·

On Tuesday after school, Lou Lou went to Marvelous Millinery, where Pea was adding the special touches to a few of the final hats—sequins and a peacock feather as her signature accent.

"Wow!" was all Lou Lou could say when Pea held up the hats for Lou Lou's inspection. She admired the feathers. "These really make it perfect!"

"As Christian Dior said, 'Feathers are lovely on a bird and glamorous on a hat,'" explained Pea.

"That's definitely true," replied Lou Lou. She tried a horticulture quote. "As Violet Petals said, 'Pretty flowers may smell like pretty dirt.'"

Pea politely didn't ask Lou Lou how that quote was related to feathers or hats, and did not point out that she never wanted to smell dirt, no matter how pretty.

"Should we get going?" Lou Lou asked. "It's almost five-thirty."

"Yes." Pea quickly put away her supplies and tidied up the workshop.

"Which hat are you bringing for the Preview?" asked Lou Lou. "One of the super-*duper*-fancy ones?" Lou Lou emphasized *duper* because most of Pea's hats were, at the very least, super-fancy.

"Abuela Josie's lucky hat, of course," Pea replied. She carefully placed the hat in a large bag and slung it over one shoulder.

"I can't wait to see her face when you show her how incredible it looks!" said Lou Lou.

"I'm also going to take the one that *I* will wear at the Bonanza. I finished it yesterday." Pea pulled a round, sky-blue, silk-covered hatbox from the cabinet. On the hatbox was a fancy sewn-on label that read *Propiedad de Peacock Pearl*. She lifted its cover to reveal a cloche made from navy velvet and trimmed with green ribbon and a peacock feather. On one side was an oversize royal-blue bow. It wasn't the most elaborate of Pea's hats, but Lou Lou could tell it was crafted with love and made from the finest of materials. When Pea modeled it over her brown hair, the blue of her eyes shimmered.

"Gorgeous!" said Lou Lou, once again awestruck by her friend's millinery talents. "What will you name it?"

"I haven't decided yet." Pea put the hat back in the box, then slung its satin braided cord over the crook of her elbow so she could close the hat shop door. "It will definitely be something extra special."

Once on the street, Lou Lou and Pea joined their El Corazón neighbors. They were all going to the same place—the Heliotrope, the girls' favorite restaurant and theater. The air was thick with excitement as everyone talked about the evening's event.

"I heard that Ella Divine is going to debut the song she wrote for the Bonanza!"

"¡Esta noche es seguro que será muy divertido!"

"It will be so amazing to see the model of the gazebo!"

It was a short walk to the Heliotrope's grand oak

doors and lighted marquee, which read in big letters: *TO-NIGHT! BICENTENNIAL BONANZA PREVIEW!* And in smaller letters below: *Complimentary slices of our famous chocolate cheesecake!* Lou Lou's mouth watered at the sign. She and Pea loved the Heliotrope's chocolate cheesecake.

Inside, the crowded theater was abuzz with activity. The evening's Preview was intended for assigning tasks to Bonanza volunteers, as well as providing a glimpse of what would happen at the Bonanza. It was like the trailer for one of Lou Lou's dad's beloved pirate movies that showed brief swashbuckling scenes, but made you wait for the film to get the whole story.

At the Preview, everyone presented a sample of the creation or performance they were working on for the upcoming celebration. In a far corner, Sarah hung one of the banners made by Lou Lou's class above an elaborate model of the gazebo that had been on display in Lou Lou's school's trophy case. In another corner, Kyle tried to stop Jupiter from gnawing on the Heliotrope's fancy velvet upholstery.

"Let's go see the Celebrar candles that Rosa ordered for the Bonanza!" Lou Lou pointed to a dark-haired older girl standing behind a candlelit table.

"And keep an eye out for my abuela! I can't wait to

give her the hat. Which reminds me . . ." Pea took her own blue hat from the box and proudly placed it on her head.

Lou Lou and Pea made their way through the crowd, stopping to get a piece of chocolate cheesecake. A voice behind Lou Lou said, "Save room for dinner. I made minestrone sloop soup. Hearty enough for my favorite first mate."

Lou Lou smiled. "Hi, Dad."

Just then, the houselights went down and the Heliotrope's manager appeared onstage in front of the heavy crimson curtain. Lou Lou and Pea turned to watch.

"Welcome and bienvenidos," the manager said. "Gracias for coming to tonight's Preview! To kick this off, let's enjoy the vocal stylings of El Corazón's favorite singer performing a piece she wrote just for the Bonanza. Please welcome the one, the only . . . Ella Divine!"

Lou Lou, Pea, and the rest of the crowd cheered. The curtain lifted and Ella Divine appeared, looking stunning. Her black hair curled elegantly around her face, her lips were painted a deep plum, and she was wearing a long gold gown tied with a wide silk sash of her signature color, emerald green. Pea nodded approvingly. Ella Divine was Pea's favorite performer, which had as much to do with her fashion sense as it did her beautiful voice.

"Good evening," said Ella Divine into the microphone. "This song is called 'Abundant Cheers for Two Hundred Years.'" Everyone was mesmerized as Ella Divine began to sing:

"They traveled many miles
Diego and dear Giles
And became the best of friends
True companions till the end
And they thought this land so pretty
So did found our lovely city
Now we celebrate our home
In our dear El Corazón
And mark our city's special day
On the twentieth of May
So raise your glass and let's say 'cheers!'
To the past two hundred years!"

At that, everyone in the Heliotrope raised their glasses in a toast. Lou Lou and Pea clinked together their pomegranate Italian sodas and joined the crowd in clapping and crying, "Bravo!" Eventually, the applause died down except for one loud slow clap.

"Spectacular, indeed!" a man's voice boomed from the back of the theater. Even though the words were complimentary, Lou Lou detected something unpleasant about the man's tone. Her ears began to tingle and she glanced at Pea, who was frowning. "But I have a small suggestion to improve your song," the voice went on. "May I join you onstage, Miss Divine?" The man sounded like he was giving an order rather than asking permission.

"It's a bit unconventional, but please do come up," Ella Divine said graciously.

When the man behind the voice approached the Heliotrope's stage, Lou Lou's ears went from pink tingly to red warm. There was something about him—Lou Lou couldn't quite put her finger on it—that screamed, *I'm up to no good!* He was tall with a pointy goatee and was wearing a satin jacket printed with gray and black diamonds, and black patent-leather shoes polished to a high shine.

Chrysanthemum, chrysanthemum, chrysanthemum, Lou Lou said three times in her head, a trick she used to calm her nerves. She didn't know who this man was or what he had to say, but Lou Lou suspected that she wasn't going to like it.

CHAPTER SEVEN
Heartbreak at the Heliotrope

"What is your name, sir?" Ella Divine asked the man when he reached the Heliotrope's stage. "I recognize you, but I can't quite place—"

"Andy Argyle." The man's dark eyes were fixed on the crowd. "Resident of Verde Valley, and"—he paused for dramatic effect—"vice-mayor of the city and Bicentennial Bonanza Boss!"

"So *that's* the vice-mayor," Lou Lou whispered.

Pea nodded. "I have a bad feeling about him, Lou Lou. Did you hear his last name? Argyle!"

Argyle, Argyle. Lou Lou racked her brain. *Where had she heard that before?*

"The rude girl in Limonero Park! Her name was Amanda Argyle and she was from Verde Valley," Pea reminded Lou Lou.

Ella Divine leaned in toward the microphone. "Welcome, Vice-Mayor Argyle. Please do share your suggestion for improving my song."

"Take out the part about your dear El Corazón," the vice-mayor said. "Instead, the song should be about Verde Valley!"

Ella Divine looked confused. "Since El Corazón is hosting this Bonanza, it doesn't make sense to change *this* song. Perhaps I can write another."

The corners of Andy Argyle's mouth turned up into a sinister smile. "What if El Corazón wasn't hosting?" His booming voice was amplified by the Heliotrope's acoustics, making it sound as if it was coming from all corners of the theater. Lou Lou's ears burned even hotter and turned fire-engine red. "Maybe our founders, Diego and Giles, had other intentions for our city's birthday celebration." There were murmurs in the crowd.

"I'm sorry. I don't understand." Ella Divine said what everyone else was thinking.

"Perhaps this will help." Andy Argyle whipped

something from his inside jacket pocket and held it up to the crowd. It was a small leather-bound book with a ribbon place marker.

"Behold, Giles Wonderwood's long-lost diary!" A gasp was heard throughout the Heliotrope.

"How interesting! I didn't know that Mr. Wonderwood kept a diary," said Ella Divine. "Wherever did you find it?"

"Daddy found it in the City Archives! I was there!" Lou Lou turned and saw Amanda Argyle standing on a chair in the back of the theater. The resemblance between the girl and her father was clear. They had the same dimpled chin and small close-set eyes. Amanda was wearing a shirt that matched her father's jacket and was similar to the diamond-print dress she had worn in the park.

"The Argyles certainly like argyle," Pea said.

Of course, thought Lou Lou. She'd learned enough from Pea's fashion passion to recognize the pattern that matched Amanda and her father's last name.

The vice-mayor made a show of clearing his throat to refocus attention on him. "Allow me to read you an excerpt from the diary," he said. He opened to the bookmarked page:

"Date: The twentieth of May.

Dearest Diary,

Diego and I declared today to be the official birthday of our new home. To celebrate, we threw a party and called it the Bonanza! We hope our descendants will hold similar celebrations in the decades to come."

Andy Argyle looked up to make sure the crowd was still listening.

"We already learned this stuff in school," Lou Lou whispered to Pea.

"I know," Pea said. "But I think there's more."

Pea was right. Andy Argyle continued to read:

"Our first official decree for our new home is that a birthday Bonanza shall be held every ten years in the EXACT SAME PLACE as our original celebration."

The vice-mayor took care to emphasize Giles's words:

"We call this special place VERDE VALLEY."

The crowd gasped again.

"Wait, what? The founders wanted the Bonanza to always happen in Verde Valley?" Lou Lou said. "No way! We never learned that in school!"

"If that's true, what does it mean for El Corazón and this year's celebration?" Pea asked. Lou Lou didn't have an answer.

Andy Argyle looked up from the diary and gave the crowd a hard, dark-eyed stare. The hint of a smug smile played on his lips.

"There you have it!" he said. "Our founders intended that Verde Valley host the Bonanza, not El Corazón, or any other neighborhood. We must obey their wishes."

"But we've always shared the honor of hosting the Bonanza!" someone in the crowd yelled. "Each neighborhood gets a turn, and this year it's El Corazón's!"

"Sharing was what happened before we knew what our founders actually wanted. From now on, all birthday Bonanzas will be in Verde Valley!" replied the vice-mayor. "Starting this year!"

"But El Corazón has been preparing for months for the Bonanza. Couldn't we make an exception?" another person asked.

"No exceptions!" Andy Argyle snapped. "It would hardly be fair to the other neighborhoods if we gave El Corazón special privileges. Besides, this is a very important Bonanza because it's the Bicentennial. That means we must do the celebration right."

"How do we know that the diary really says what you claim?" someone else asked.

"Because I say so and I'm the vice-mayor!" boomed Andy Argyle. "But if you don't trust me, you can come to the City Archives in City Hall and I will show it to you myself." It seemed like he had an answer for everything. "The Bonanza will relocate to Verde Valley! And since the gazebo was meant for the host neighborhood, it now belongs to Verde Valley as well!" Andy Argyle rubbed his palms together when he said the word *gazebo* and sneered the way Amanda had in the park.

Lou Lou could hardly believe her ears. Relocate the

Bonanza? And the gazebo? After El Corazón had worked so hard? She looked at Pea in disbelief. "What will happen to the honeysuckle? The performances? Oh Pea, your beautiful hats?" She was about to get another unwelcome answer.

"In case there is any confusion, let me quickly remind you of the official city rules for this year's celebration." The vice-mayor reached into his inside jacket pocket again, pulled out a piece of paper, and began to read aloud: *"In addition to choosing the location for the gazebo, the host neighborhood will be in charge of all Bonanza crafts, creations, and performance plans."* Andy Argyle looked at the crowd triumphantly. "You will hand over all of El Corazón's Bonanza preparations this weekend in Limonero Park. Otherwise, I will forbid you from even attending the celebration!"

"It's not fair," cried someone in the crowd.

"¡Hemos trabajado muy duro!" someone else said.

Lou Lou thought about all the time and effort she and Juan had put into the honeysuckle. It was nothing compared to Pea's hard work on the hats. She looked over at Pea, whose blue eyes were filling with tears. Lou Lou took her best friend's hand and gave it a comforting squeeze.

"But Daddy, I don't want to wait until the weekend. I

want a Bonanza hat NOW! You told me I could have one NOW!" Amanda whined. All eyes turned back toward her as, much to Lou Lou's horror, she pointed at Pea's beautiful blue hat. Pea put a hand on it protectively.

"Of course, darling," Andy Argyle said to Amanda. He looked at Pea. "Hand over the hat, little girl!" he commanded.

"Now, just you wait right here. There's no reason my daughter has to give that up!" Lou Lou saw Pea's father, Henry Pearl, in the crowd.

"Indeed, there is a reason. As I already told you, Verde Valley is now in charge of everything," Andy Argyle said curtly. "Including the hats!"

"But . . ." Pea's lower lip quivered.

"Can't we let her keep at least one one . . . ?" Lou Lou recognized Mr. Vila's voice.

"No exceptions!" Andy Argyle boomed again. Lou Lou noticed Amanda Argyle moving toward them through the crowd.

"Gimme!" she said, and lunged at Pea, who was frozen in shock.

"DON'T YOU DARE TOUCH THAT HAT!" Lou Lou shouted. "IT BELONGS TO MY BEST FRIEND!"

Amanda paused for a moment. "Not everyone gets to have a best friend," she said, her voice low.

Lou Lou sprang into action, blocking Amanda's way. But it was no use. Amanda was a good three inches taller than Lou Lou and easily reached over Lou Lou's curls to snatch the hat from Pea's head. The peacock feather tore off and fluttered to the floor. Pea clasped her hands to her chest.

"This actually belongs to Verde Valley! Fair and square!" crowed Amanda, squishing the bow on the hat as she mashed it onto her own head. Amanda reached down to grab the hatbox at Pea's feet, as well as the bag with Abuela Josie's hat.

"Wait! That's my abuela's lucky hat! It's special and she needs it! Please!"

Amanda gave no sign of hearing Pea's plea. She stomped back into the crowd, and Lou Lou watched the words *Propiedad de Peacock Pearl* disappear.

With that, the Bicentennial Bonanza dreams of Lou Lou, Pea, and the rest of El Corazón went dark alongside the Heliotrope's stage lights.

CHAPTER EIGHT
Giles . . . Diary . . . Fake

The Bonanza commotion at the Heliotrope died down and all that was left was a cloud of sadness. As everyone packed up what they'd brought for the Preview, Lou Lou turned to Pea.

"I can't believe they took it from us!" she said.

"Me neither," Pea said quietly. "My abuela will be devastated. And I hadn't even named mine yet." Lou Lou had been talking about the Bonanza, but Pea was mourning her hats.

"We've got to get them back for you!" Lou Lou said. She thought quickly about how to do this, as she couldn't stand seeing her best friend so sad. "Maybe we can call

Mayor Montoya and ask her for help," Lou Lou suggested.

"But we don't know how to reach her," Pea replied. "Only the vice-mayor knows."

"Right," Lou Lou said. "We could *try* to talk to Andy Argyle. Sometimes mean people turn out to have hearts of gold." Lou Lou found it hard to believe that the vice-mayor could have a heart of gold or even of brass. But she didn't have a better idea.

"Okay." Pea scanned the crowd. "Afterward, I have to find my abuela and break the horrible news about her lucky hat." A tear rolled down Pea's cheek.

Lou Lou glanced over at her parents. Her mom was helping Sarah roll up the banner, and her dad was chasing one of Kyle's disobedient goats and yelling, "Avast, you furry beast!" It would be a few minutes before they wondered about Lou Lou's whereabouts, so she took Pea's hand and moved through the crowd toward the vice-mayor. Andy Argyle was surrounded by an unhappy group of people from El Corazón, including Pea's parents. Friends and neighbors patted Pea's shoulder sympathetically as they passed.

"Sorry, niña," said Clara the mailwoman.

"This is truly a fashion tragedy. Your hats are gorgeous!" said Thomas, the owner of Sparkle 'N Clean.

Even in her disheartened state, Pea still mustered weak *thank you*s.

Lou Lou and Pea climbed the stairs to the stage just in time to see Andy Argyle throw out his hands to part the crowd and quickly exit stage left.

"Shoot! Where did he go?" asked Lou Lou.

"Over there." Pea pointed at the Argyles, who were disappearing through a door marked EXIT/SALIDA.

"Quick, let's follow them," said Lou Lou, hurrying to the exit with Pea close behind. Lou Lou pushed open the door and felt a blast of crisp night air. She stepped outside and saw the Argyles sitting in their nearby parked car. Lou Lou was about to call out hello when instinct told her to keep quiet and she ducked behind the Heliotrope's trash bin, pulling Pea after her.

"What are we doing back here?" Pea asked. She looked horrified by the rainbow of discarded drink umbrellas, crumpled napkins, and half-eaten pieces of chocolate cheesecake in the trash.

"More importantly, who doesn't finish their chocolate cheesecake?" asked Lou Lou.

"I thought we were going to talk to the vice-mayor," Pea said.

"Shhh, let's listen."

The Argyles had the windows down in their car, and were talking loudly as they flipped through radio stations.

". . . it actually worked and they believed . . ." Amanda said before her voice was drowned out by Latin pop.

"Gazebo!" boomed Andy. He was interrupted by a radio opera tenor, and all Lou Lou could hear was "back-yard" and "precious little neighborhood."

"Jealous of us for once . . ." The sound of the local weather report cut Amanda off.

"Giles . . . diary . . . fake" were the only other words of Andy Argyle's that Lou Lou caught over the smooth jazz station.

"Let's go. I want to admire my pretty new hat in my big mirror! I can't wait to try on all the others, too." The Argyles had turned off the radio, so Amanda came through loud and clear. Andy Argyle started the car and they peeled off into the darkness.

"Did you hear that, Pea?"

"I most certainly did. As if Amanda could truly appreciate the beauty of my hats," Pea said.

"I'm sure that's true, but I was talking about what Andy Argyle said," replied Lou Lou. "'Giles . . . diary . . . fake.' What do you think he meant? Maybe Giles is a fake person who never really came to our city? No, that can't be right. Could it be that Giles's diary is actually a fake?"

"I don't know," said Pea. She thought for a moment.

"It's a possibility, but we didn't hear everything he said, so we can't be sure."

"The vice-mayor could be lying about the founders' decree that the Bonanza must be in Verde Valley!" Lou Lou guessed.

"Can we move away from this trash bin now?" asked Pea. "A maraschino cherry just missed falling on my head." When Lou Lou and Pea emerged from their hiding spot and were a safe distance from the trash cans, Pea wiped her hands with her pale blue handkerchief and smoothed the wrinkles in her dress. Then she said, "So the Argyles faked the diary so they could move the Bonanza?"

"Exactly! It's the *Bicentennial Bonanza* after all! It's one of the coolest things to happen in two hundred years. Andy Argyle even said something about a backyard. He's probably thrilled about moving the Bonanza to his own backyard, as in, his neighborhood."

Pea nodded. "Plus, my hats will go to Verde Valley," she said quietly. "I didn't even have time to finish them all. No one from El Corazón will get to wear one at the Bonanza and they'll be lost to me forever."

"And the gazebo, too!" added Lou Lou. "What should we do now? Should we tell someone what we heard?"

"Slow down, Lou Lou." Pea held up her hands. "We don't know for sure that the diary is a fake or even whether that's what Vice-Mayor Argyle said. So we shouldn't jump to any conclusions." Pea was practical about these things. If conclusions were a pool, Lou Lou would be constantly getting wet.

Lou Lou took a breath. "And even if we were certain, we don't have any proof." She brightened. "But we sure are good at finding it!" Lou Lou thought back to their excellent work on the mural mystery. "If it means we get to keep the Bonanza and your hats, then we have to investigate."

"I agree," said Pea. "But let's start tomorrow. I'm exhausted. It's been an eventful evening and not in a good way." Pea held open the back door of the Heliotrope for Lou Lou. As usual, Pea was right. It would be best to get some rest and make a plan the next day. Still, Lou Lou couldn't put Andy Argyle's words, *Giles, diary, fake,* out of her head. If the diary really was a fake, she and Pea were going to prove it!

CHAPTER NINE
Lou Lou and Pea to the Rescue Again!

The people of El Corazón were dismayed after the heartbreak at the Heliotrope. The neighborhood went from bustling and enthusiastic to quiet and gloomy. There were no more excited discussions of Bonanza preparations on the street and in the shops. In school the next day, Kyle never once mentioned his space goats, and Danielle's snooty-girl posse didn't do a single shimmy. Even the day was dreary and gray, as if the weather was sympathizing with El Corazón.

Pea, in particular, was grief-stricken over the loss of her hats. The day after the Preview was only a Wednesday, but Lou Lou called an emergency PSPP to comfort her friend and discuss the situation. Emergency PSPPs were very rare. In the history of PSPP, there had only been one other, when a raccoon had destroyed all of Lou Lou's tomato plants right before the salsa festival.

When she arrived at the SS *Lucky Alley* for emergency PSPP, Pea's eyes were puffy and she was quieter than usual. She barely managed a weak, polite, "Thank you, my dear," when Lou Lou served her tea in her favorite blue teacup as they sat together in Lou Lou's backyard garden.

"Did you talk to your abuela last night?" Lou Lou asked.

Pea nodded. "She was so sad about her hat. She tried to explain to Vice-Mayor Argyle that she's had it for ages, so it really belongs to her, not to the Bonanza, but he wouldn't listen."

"¡Qué piña!" Lou Lou said.

"I think you mean 'Qué pena,'" said Pea. "You wanted to say, 'What a pity!' but you said, 'What a pineapple!'"

"Got it," said Lou Lou, feeling a little silly.

"I even saw Abuela Josie's eyes tear up when I told her what had happened." Pea continued her story. "Of course, she said it was okay and gave me a big hug, but I know she was just trying to make me feel better. It's all my fault that her hat is gone. I never should have let that . . . that . . ." Pea searched for a word. She wasn't good at not being nice. ". . . rather unkind Amanda take it!" Now, Pea's eyes began to fill with tears.

"It's not your fault, Pea!" Lou Lou said. "Don't ever say that! It's those awful Argyles. And don't worry, we're going to find a way to stop them!" She had an idea. "Since you're related to Diego, maybe your abuela has something to help with our diary investigation?"

"To contradict what Vice-Mayor Argyle said? If she did, I'm sure she would have mentioned it," replied Pea.

"Not if she doesn't know about it. Sometimes people don't realize they have a clue right in front of their eyes. Remember the details on the murals? You have to be looking for clues, like we were."

"I know she has a few old family things in her attic." Pea tucked a stray piece of brown hair behind her ear. "We could visit her after school on Thursday and take a look. That is, if you don't need to water your honeysuckle."

Pea's mention of the honeysuckle made Lou Lou's ears prickle with heat. She'd been trying not to worry about whether Andy Argyle planned to uproot the plants from

Limonero Park, but she felt like she might burst if she didn't talk about it soon. Luckily, Pea knew her well.

"I know you're concerned about the honeysuckle, Lou Lou. You don't have to keep quiet about it for my sake," Pea said.

"They better not take it! It's not right, Pea! Particularly since I know the Argyles are lying! Juan and I worked so hard to plant that honeysuckle, and the light in Limonero Park is perfect! What if Verde Valley is full of vicious caterpillars and canker disease?" Lou Lou felt better. She was no longer an overfull balloon about to pop.

"Verde Valley is not a bad place. They also have a pretty park, and the Verde Valley kids who go to my school are nice," Pea said.

"You're right," Lou Lou agreed. "Andy Argyle is the devious thief, not Verde Valley."

Pea took a delicate bite of her lemon scone. "I agree that it seems *really* suspicious that Vice-Mayor Argyle would find the diary now, right before the Bonanza." She looked thoughtful as she took another nibble. "Even though I was distracted by the close encounter with the trash bin, I remember hearing Amanda say 'It actually worked and they believed it.' Which sounds a little like they made up a story to fool everyone."

"It sounds *a lot* like they made up a story to fool everyone, Pea," Lou Lou said.

"What will we do if Abuela Josie doesn't have anything that will help?" Pea asked.

"We'll have to actually examine the diary to see if there's any way to prove it's a fake," replied Lou Lou. "But I don't know yet how we'll do that without Vice-Mayor Argyle knowing," she admitted. "Plan A is to talk to Abuela Josie. Examining the diary is plan B. And I haven't gotten past A yet."

Just then, Lou Lou's foghorn doorbell rang. She hurried to answer it and found Rosa on the stoop wearing a purple dress with beaded cuffs.

"Hola, Rosa!" Lou Lou said. "What are you doing here?" Lou Lou remembered Pea's lessons in manners. "I mean, I'm delighted to see you. Pea is in my garden. You are just in time to join us for PSPP tea." Rosa followed Lou Lou out to the backyard.

"Buenas tardes, Rosa." Pea brightened at the sight of the Candle Lady.

"Hello, Peacock. Lou Lou, your garden looks beautiful!" Rosa said.

Lou Lou grinned. "I can't disagree!" The spring flowers in the Bouquet Blooms section of her garden were

out in their colorful glory, and it was almost time for the odd blooms in the Summer Weirds section to come up. Punky, Lou Lou's rowdy rebel variety camellia that grew in the shade of the backyard avocado tree, was thriving.

"Would you care for some tea and a scone, Rosa?" Pea asked.

"No, thank you. No puedo quedarme mucho tiempo. I just came by to bring you a Celebrar candle," Rosa said. She took a red candle from her purse and set it on the table. There was a picture of a party hat and a noisemaker on the glass holder.

"This is a Bonanza candle, right? Aren't you supposed to give it to Verde Valley?" Lou Lou asked.

"I ordered a few extras, so no one will miss it." Rosa winked.

"Gracias, it's lovely. But unfortunately we don't have much to celebrate anymore," Pea said sadly.

"Don't lose hope! You never know what might happen, chicas. You two always find a way to work things out." Rosa smiled. "I must return to the candle shop. It's almost Helado's suppertime, and I will have a very hungry bunny on my hands if I'm late!" Lou Lou and Pea said adiós and Rosa left through the side gate.

Lou Lou waited until Rosa was gone, then looked at

her best friend. "Did you hear that? She said we 'always find a way to work things out.' Funny that we were just talking about a plan to do exactly that. It's a sign! We have to prove that the diary is a fake as soon as possible so we can fix this fiasco!"

Lou Lou thought of something else. "Pea, in the meantime, I think we should make a new hat for Abuela Josie!" Today was clearly a day for positive planning.

"That's a nice thought, Lou Lou, but I don't think I could replace the hat my abuelo gave her," said Pea.

"It doesn't have to be a replacement. We'll make her a totally new hat. The old one would still be special, but the new one could be, too!"

"That might make her feel a bit better," Pea agreed. "And me too."

"We'll figure out what styles and colors she likes," said Lou Lou.

"But it should be a surprise," added Pea.

"¡Absolutamente!" Lou Lou replied. This was one of her favorite Spanish words because it was so much fun to say. Lou Lou stood on one of the wobbly metal garden chairs and cleared her throat like she was about to give an important speech. "I am going to make a decree just like the founders. We will make a new hat for Abuela

Josie! We will reclaim the Bicentennial Bonanza! I hereby declare"—Lou Lou paused and waved her hands in the air—"Lou Lou and Pea to the rescue again!"

"You sound like Kyle when he's excited about one of his Comet Cop missions." Pea laughed and Lou Lou joined in. She wasn't certain they could get back the Bonanza for their neighborhood. But for now, she was just happy that she could cheer up Pea.

CHAPTER TEN
Abuela Josie's Attic

On Thursday after school, Lou Lou and Pea went to see Abuela Josie. Pea's abuela lived a few doors down from the Pearls in a little stucco house with a red roof. On Abuela Josie's front door hung a brass horse's-head knocker, and a horseshoe overhead brought good luck.

Pea knocked and her abuela opened the door almost immediately. "¡Hola, mijas! You're just in time for pan dulces."

"¡Qué estupendo!" Pea smiled at the mention of sweet treats, and she and Lou Lou both gave Abuela Josie a hug.

Inside, Abuela Josie's house was filled with horse decorations and rodeo memorabilia. There were needle-point horse pillows on the couch, a horse-head vase, and photographs from Abuela Josie's vaquera days. Lou Lou paused to look at a photo of a young Abuela Josie at a rodeo. She was wearing her lucky hat, and Pea's abuelo—a man with a bright smile who had passed away when Pea was little—had his arm around Abuela Josie's shoulders.

The cozy kitchen smelled like baking and a plate of pan dulces rested on the table. Lou Lou and Pea sat down and Abuela Josie handed them steaming mugs of hot chocolate spiced with cinnamon and cayenne pepper. As she waited for hers to cool, Lou Lou glanced at the Bonanza program on the fridge.

"I couldn't bear to take it down!" Abuela Josie said. "I was so excited about the Bonanza. The last time El Corazón hosted, I was just a teenager, and this year is muy, muy especial because it's the Bicentennial. And we were supposed to get the lovely gazebo for Limonero Park . . . this whole thing is very sad."

"Yes," Lou Lou agreed. "I'm sorry about your lucky hat, Abuela Josie." Pea stared into her mug. Abuela Josie put her hand over Pea's and gave it a squeeze.

< 87 >

"Thank you, Lou Lou. I can't say I'm not upset. But now that El Corazón has lost the Bonanza, I won't be performing my stunt anyways, hat or no hat!"

"That's so unfair! You've been practicing for months." Lou Lou's ears prickled with heat. She'd hoped Andy Argyle might make an exception for Abuela Josie's performance since no one from Verde Valley could learn her stunt. But Lou Lou remembered the harsh words the vice-mayor had repeated at the Heliotrope: *no exceptions.*

"Eso si que es." Abuela Josie sighed. Lou Lou gave Pea a meaningful look. It was time to start their diary investigation.

"Abuela, I'm doing some research for a Bonanza history project." Pea chose her words carefully. She didn't want to lie to her abuela, but Lou Lou and Pea had decided not to reveal their suspicions that the diary was a fake until they had more proof. No adult could tell them not to snoop if no one knew they were investigating in the first place! "May I look at the old family things in the attic?"

"Sounds interesting! Of course you may," Abuela Josie replied. Lou Lou was relieved that Pea's abuela didn't ask for specifics about the "project." "There is a box of heirlooms up there somewhere. I haven't opened it in years, but you're welcome to take a peek. I'm sure every-thing could use a little organizing and dusting, too!" Abuela Josie winked at Pea who would be excited about cleaning and tidying.

When they'd finished eating, Lou Lou and Pea picked up their mugs to go to the attic.

"Which do you like better, Abuela Josie? The red mug or the yellow mug?" Lou Lou asked. Pea raised her eye-brows, but nodded when Lou Lou scratched her head in a secret gesture. In order to make a new hat for Pea's abuela, they needed to know what colors she liked.

"Definitely red," replied Abuela Josie, though she looked puzzled at the question.

"Do you prefer felt to leather, or vice versa?" Pea asked.

"That's an odd question. But leather, I suppose," Abuela Josie replied. "I'd rather wear riding boots than slippers."

Lou Lou and Pea climbed a narrow staircase up to the small attic at the top of the house. It had slanted ceilings and one tiny window that let in light, revealing an array of items scattered on the floor and on built-in shelves. The attic reminded Lou Lou a little of the crow's nest, except it was filled with boxes and not nautical-themed.

Lou Lou and Pea looked through chipped plates, dusty books, and trophies from Abuela Josie's vaquera days. Lou Lou hadn't thought it possible for Abuela Josie to have even more horse-themed trinkets and housewares, but she was wrong. There was a large ceramic horse lamp that Pea carefully dusted, brass horse figurines, and rodeo scene snow globes.

Pea organized issues of *Modern Equestrian* by date while Lou Lou glanced at labels on boxes. They were in Spanish, so she read them aloud to Pea.

"*Espuelas.*"

"Spurs," Pea translated.

"*Aceite de Silla de Montar.*"

"Saddle oil."

"*Diamantes de Imitación.*"

"Rhinestones."

Lou Lou checked the next three boxes: "*Diamantes de Imitación, Diamantes de Imitación,* and *Más Diamantes de Imitación.* At least we know where to find rhinestones for our next art project."

"Take a few for Abuela Josie's hat!" Pea said.

Lou Lou grabbed a handful of the glittering jewels and

put them in her pocket. She stood on her tippy toes to see the label on the top box in the stack. *"Herencias Familiares."*

"Family heirlooms!" said Pea. "That's the one!" She helped Lou Lou bring the box to the floor. Lou Lou took a deep breath and Pea lifted off the top. Inside, the box was filled with pottery, silver, and other small treasures.

"There's got to be something helpful in here!" Lou Lou said.

"I hope so! At the very least, everything could use a good cleaning," replied Pea.

Lou Lou and Pea dove in, taking items from the box one by one. There was a water jug painted with colorful birds, a locket with an engraved honeysuckle blossom and the words *Te amo*, and even a love letter from Diego to his wife, Catalina. Pea polished all the silver to a high shine. The box was filled with interesting and pretty things, but Lou Lou and Pea were disappointed that there wasn't anything useful to their investigation.

Lou Lou sighed. "I guess we'll need to examine the diary. Nothing in here will save the Bonanza."

"Or any of my hats, including Abuela Josie's lucky one," Pea added quietly.

"I know. I'm sorry, Pea. But we're not giving up! And at least we're making Abuela Josie a new hat."

"Sí," Pea said, though she still sounded sad. Lou Lou knew that a new hat for Abuela Josie, while a good idea, couldn't take away the heartbreak of losing all the beautiful hats on which Pea had worked so hard.

Pea put the top on the *Herencias Familiares* box and Lou Lou helped her return it to the stack. As they headed for the stairs, the end of a bedsheet caught on Lou Lou's foot and she pulled it to the floor, revealing a large, ornately framed painting of a dignified-looking dark-haired man in a fancy red coat sitting on a horse.

"You found the painting of Diego!" Abuela Josie appeared at the top of the stairs. "I came up to show that to you."

Lou Lou recognized their city's founder from the mural. "He's very handsome," she said.

"Yes. And speaking of good looks, that's Tío Diego's beautiful sorrel mare." Abuela Josie pointed at the reddish-brown horse in the painting.

"What's a sorrel?" asked Pea.

"It's a plant," Lou Lou replied. Then she realized that didn't make sense when sorrel was used to describe a horse.

"True, but for horses, it's actually a color," Abuela Josie said.

"I'll remember that," said Pea. "I don't think it's in my color book." Pea had a book called *The Definitive Book of Color.* It had proven useful for her art and for solving mysteries.

"Did you find what you were looking for up here?" asked Abuela Josie.

"We found some neat family things," replied Lou Lou. *But nothing that will prove the Argyles are lying,* she thought. "Oh and these." Lou Lou pulled the rhinestones from her pocket.

"May we use them for a fashion project?" Pea asked.

"Absolutely, Nieta! I think you should take this with you, as well." She pointed at the painting. "Your tío Diego can remind you that you will always be a part of our city's history, no matter which neighborhood is hosting the Bonanza. You too, Lou Lou."

"Gracias, Abuela!" Pea gave her grandmother another hug. Lou Lou joined in with her own hug and thank-you.

"By the way, Abuela Josie, do you like ostriches or peacocks better?" Lou Lou asked.

"Faux fur or tulle?" Pea said.

"Silver or gold?" asked Lou Lou.

"You two are full of strange questions today," replied Abuela Josie. "Silver. Faux fur. And definitely peacocks." She smiled at Pea.

Lou Lou took one end of the large painting and helped Pea carry it down the stairs. As they left Abuela Josie's house, Lou Lou looked at Diego's brown eyes and serious but kind face. She could almost hear his voice saying, *Salven la Bonanza, Lou Lou Bombay y Peacock Pearl!*

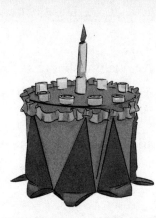

CHAPTER ELEVEN
Superior Honeysuckle

The next day's non-emergency PSPP was the second somber PSPP of the week. The arrival of Friday meant they were one day closer to El Corazón's handover of Bonanza preparations to Verde Valley. To cheer themselves up, Lou Lou and Pea decided to have PSPP at Marvelous Millinery so they could work on Abuela Josie's new hat.

Lou Lou sipped her tea while she watched Pea stitch together red leather to make the top piece of the vaquera hat. "How can I help?" she asked.

"You can put some rhinestones on the brim," replied Pea. Lou Lou washed scone crumbs from her hands, then Pea showed her how to attach the jewels.

As they worked, they discussed their investigation. But they didn't come up with any great ideas for examining Giles's diary.

"Maybe Andy Argyle will bring the diary to the park tomorrow and we can read it when he has his back turned," Lou Lou suggested.

"Maybe." Pea didn't sound convinced. She opened a bag of faux-fur pom-poms and held up a few against the leather.

"Those are pretty," said Lou Lou.

"I'm not sure they're right for the hat," Pea replied. "But they are lovely accents. As Karl Lagerfeld said, 'You cannot fake chic but you can be chic and fake fur.'"

· ⟩⟩ · ⟨⟨ ·

The next morning, Lou Lou followed her usual Saturday routine. By seven-thirty, she was awake, dressed, and down the crow's nest's rope ladder. After Lou Lou visited her garden, she sat down to breakfast at the SS *Lucky Alley* kitchen table made from the hull of a small boat. Lou Lou and her parents discussed the Bonanza over banana pancakes.

"It certainly is tragic," said Lou Lou's mom. "Everyone

in El Corazón was looking forward to hosting the celebration, and we've spent so much time preparing." She glanced at a box filled with her origami birthday cakes that she would now have to give to Verde Valley. "And poor Peacock losing her beautiful hats! What will happen to the honeysuckle, honey?" Lou Lou's mom didn't seem to realize that sounded funny.

"I'm not sure yet," said Lou Lou. She checked the antique chronometer on the shelf above the stove. "But I'll know soon. It's time to go to Limonero Park!"

"Aye, aye, matey!" said Lou Lou's dad. "You go ahead. We'll be there once I finish baking catamaran cookies."

Lou Lou grabbed her red hoodie from the ship's-mast coatrack. "Great! I'm sure Pea will be happy to have fresh cookies when we get back." She knew Pea loved the sailboat-shaped sugar cookies topped with blue and white sprinkles.

"Before you go, Lou Lou, I have a joke for you," her dad said. "What kind of sweater did the pirate wear?"

"I don't know, Dad." Lou Lou was reminded of Kyle's bad jokes.

"Arrrgyle, of course!" her dad replied. Lou Lou mustered a grin before she shut the door behind her.

When Lou Lou reached Limonero Park, it was already

busy with the handover of the Bonanza preparations. Many of Lou Lou's neighbors were there, just like at the Heliotrope. But unlike the Heliotrope gathering, there was no festive feeling in the air. Instead the people of El Corazón moved about the park with sad eyes and heavy hearts. Lou Lou saw Kyle giving his goats to another ruddy-faced boy.

"Please take good care of them, Tommy," Kyle said. He hugged Jupiter around the neck, and the goat nibbled on Kyle's hair.

Nearby, Danielle Desserts and her snooty-girl posse were teaching a group of Verde Valley girls to do the Sugar Mountain Sisters' Shimmy.

"Sashay, sashay, jazz hands!" Danielle commanded. "No, no, no! I said 'jazz hands' not 'spaghetti fingers'! Try it again!" Even though Danielle was being her usual bossy self, Lou Lou sympathized with the sorrowful note in Danielle's voice. She'd worked hard on the Sugar Mountain Sisters' Shimmy, and it couldn't be easy to have to give up dancing in its debut performance.

Before she tracked down Juan to ask about the honeysuckle, Lou Lou looked for Pea. It didn't take long to find her best friend. Pea stood forlornly between two lemon trees, surrounded by a multicolored sea of hatboxes and bags.

"Hi," said Lou Lou, putting her arm around Pea's shoulders. "¿Cómo estás?"

"Bien," Pea replied, but from her sorrowful tone and her quivering chin, Lou Lou didn't believe that she was doing well.

"Where's Mr. Vila?" Lou Lou asked.

"He went to get the rest of the hats. In the meantime, I'm waiting to give these to Verde Valley." She nodded at the boxes and bags. Following Pea's gaze, Lou Lou saw the hats Pea had named Lady Lou Lou's Luxury and Bombay Bazaar. Lou Lou felt a familiar warmth in her ears. She definitely believed the diary was a fake, the Bonanza was stolen, and Verde Valley had no right to take Pea's beloved hats. But even if the Argyles weren't lying, Lou Lou still felt upset that Pea would lose her hats.

"Have you checked on your honeysuckle yet?" Pea asked.

"No. I wanted to check on *you* first," Lou Lou replied.

"I'll be all right. I promise," Pea said.

Lou Lou scanned the park to find Juan. He was over near the long row of honeysuckle talking to Andy Argyle, and from the way Juan was waving his hands, things didn't look good.

"We can't just dig up the plants without damaging

them," Lou Lou heard Juan say as she approached. He gave the shovel in Andy Argyle's hand a dirty look.

"We'll have to take our chances, won't we? The honeysuckle belongs to Verde Valley now," replied the vice-mayor. Lou Lou marched to Juan's side, not bothering to say any *chrysanthemum*s or try to cool her fiery ears.

"But—" she began.

"What do we have here? A little girl who wants to get her way, just like that hat girl at the Heliotrope. El Corazón seems to be filled with them." This made Lou Lou even angrier. She hated being called little. "No BUTS," Andy Argyle added.

"I don't want their stupid plants, Daddy." Amanda Argyle stomped over to her father. She was wearing Pea's hat again. Lou Lou hoped Pea couldn't see Amanda. Pea's day was already bad enough. "I took some cuttings when I was here before. We can grow far superior Verde Valley honeysuckle." Amanda twirled her braids around her fingers and looked smug.

"'Superior'? Did you say *superior*?" Lou Lou said. "And do you really think you have enough time—" Juan put a hand on her arm, and Lou Lou got the message. Silence might mean they could save their plants.

"If you say so, darling daughter," said Andy Argyle. "You can keep your silly honeysuckle," he said to Juan and Lou Lou. "Come on, Amanda. Let's go find some of the more interesting Bonanza creations." Andy Argyle spun on a shiny-shoed heel.

Lou Lou helped Juan water the honeysuckle and went to rejoin Pea. But before she reached the other side of the park, she nearly ran headlong into Jeremy.

"Whoooaaa there!" Jeremy put up his hands to avoid a collision. He backed up a step to peer down at Lou Lou, and one of the red spikes of his hair flopped over. "Hello, my clumsy friend."

"You're the one who wasn't looking where you were going," said Lou Lou.

"You've got a point. Sorry about that," Jeremy said. "With all that's going on today, I guess I was distracted. It's such a bummer to lose all of this." He looked around at the park.

"It's so unfair! Even if the Bonanza does belong in Verde Valley, the Argyles are really taking this too far,"

Lou Lou replied. "Anyway, Pea and I have our suspicions about their story and the diary. We've decided to investigate!"

"Uh-oh, the Argyles better watch out!" said Jeremy. "When it comes to investigations, Lou Lou Bombay and Peacock Pearl mean business."

"What will happen with the caracoles contest?" Lou Lou asked. "Can you still enter?"

"I hope so!" said Jeremy. "It's always been open to the whole city, not just the Bonanza host neighborhood, and I haven't heard any different. Hey, do you and Peacock want to come over later? I've tried some new ingredients and I wanna know whatcha think. You can also tell me more about this investigation."

"Sure!" Lou Lou decided that her dad's catamaran cookies could wait. "Pea will need some cheering up, and caracoles might just do the trick."

"¡Excelente! Hasta luego!" Jeremy loped off toward the far edge of the park.

When she rejoined Pea, the hatboxes and bags were gone and Kyle was showing Pea his cosmic kung fu. "And then a crater chop." Kyle waved his hand through the air. "Followed by a shooting-star side kick." Kyle threw a leg out to the right.

"Hi, Lou Lou Bombay," Kyle said. "I was just showing Peacock what I would have done if I'd been here when they took her hats away."

"I'm so sorry, Pea." Lou Lou hugged her friend.

"Vice-Mayor Argyle said he would keep them himself until the Bonanza so Amanda could try on every one." Pea wiped her eyes with her handkerchief.

"Maybe a snack and working on our diary investigation will make you feel better!" Lou Lou told Pea about Jeremy's taste-testing offer.

"Sounds good," Pea agreed.

"Did you say 'investigation'? That's right up my cosmic alley. Nobody handles an investigation better than Comet Cop!" Kyle said.

Lou Lou rolled her eyes. "I suppose you can come, too, Kyle."

CHAPTER TWELVE
Planning and Pastries

Lou Lou found her parents at the park to tell them her plans. She promised to be home for afternoon catamaran cookies. Then she, Pea, and Kyle headed off to Jeremy's little green house. When they arrived, Jeremy answered the door wearing a pink apron with ruffles. Lou Lou couldn't help but laugh. She wasn't used to seeing Jeremy wear any color, let alone pink.

"Hey, this is my favorite apron," Jeremy said. "It complements my complexion, if I do say so myself."

Pea nodded approvingly. "Christian Dior said pink 'is the color of happiness.'"

"I hope you don't mind that Kyle came along," Lou Lou said.

"Naw, not at all. The more the merrier. And my parents are still at the park, so I could use an extra taste tester."

Lou Lou had never been inside Jeremy's family's new house, but given his love of black, she'd assumed it would be dark and gloomy. Instead, his home was bright, colorful, and cheery, from the paisley-print curtains to the peach-colored walls. Jeremy noticed her looking around.

"Yeah, my family doesn't share my spooky demeanor." He winked.

On the counter in Jeremy's sunny yellow kitchen was a platter piled high with caracoles. "That there's three of you is actually perfecto!" Jeremy said. "I have three different kinds so you can each try one. I won't reveal the secret ingredient until you taste them."

Jeremy handed out napkins and the pastries with a "ta da!" for each. He watched closely as Lou Lou, Pea, and Kyle took their first bites. "Blech!" Lou Lou spit her bite into her napkin. Pea gave her a horrified look. "What's in this, Jeremy? It's . . . well . . . terrible."

"That one has beef bouillon. I thought the secret might be to add something savory, but I guess not."

"*Definitely* not," replied Lou Lou, who couldn't even think of a way to be nice about the awful caracol.

"I'll try yours," Kyle said between mouthfuls of his pastry.

Lou Lou handed it over. "Be my guest." She glanced at Pea. She'd taken a bite from her own caracol, but had stopped chewing. Her cheeks looked flushed and her blue eyes were wide.

"Pea!" Lou Lou exclaimed. "Are you okay?"

Pea shook her head.

"Oh no!" Jeremy rushed to get Pea a glass of milk. She took a big gulp. "That's the one with habanero. I guess it's a bit too spicy."

"Just a tad," Pea croaked.

"I'll eat it." Kyle took the rest of Pea's caracol.

"How's yours, Kyle?" Jeremy asked.

"Not like Señora Basa's, but still delicious," Kyle said.

"What's the secret ingredient in that one?" asked Lou Lou.

"Sauerkraut," Jeremy replied.

"Ick!" Lou Lou couldn't help exclaiming. Like beef bouillon and caracoles, sauerkraut and caracoles was not a combination that sounded good.

"I told you, I was trying out savory since I've already tested every sweet ingredient I can think of. But I guess it didn't work."

"Works for me," Kyle said. He'd finished his own cara-col and was moving on to Lou Lou's.

"I'm sure you'll figure it out eventually, Jeremy." Lou Lou tried to be encouraging even though she wasn't certain this was true. Pea nodded and smiled weakly after another gulp of milk.

"'Eventually' better be soon because the Bonanza is coming right up," said Jeremy. "It sure would be nice to win the caracoles contest for El Corazón after this horrible week! Speaking of which, tell me about this investigation of yours."

Lou Lou and Pea—once she regained her powers of speech after the habanero caracol—told Jeremy and Kyle about the snippets of the Argyles' conversation they'd overheard outside the Heliotrope, their guess that the diary might be a fake, and their suspicion that the Bonanza was actually stolen. Kyle was a bit of a tattletale, but Lou Lou trusted he would keep quiet because he wanted his space goats back. And also to impress Pea.

"Our plan is to examine the diary and see if we can find anything that proves it's a fake," Lou Lou explained. "Maybe there are mistakes or maybe the diary is really just a bunch of blank pages except for the made-up part that Andy Argyle read at the Heliotrope."

"That sounds easy," Jeremy replied. "The vice-mayor said that people could see the diary in the City Archives, right?"

"Yes. But his exact words were 'You can come to the City Archives in City Hall and I will show it to you myself.'" Pea had a great memory. She could sing the words to songs from nursery school and perfectly recite messages from old birthday cards.

"Yeah, and there's no way Andy Argyle is going to show us anything that proves anything," Lou Lou said. "We need to look at the diary on our own."

"How will you get into the City Archives? It's not the kind of place you can just casually visit on your way to the bodega. No sera fácil." Jeremy was right. They all knew from school field trips that the City Archives were behind a locked door and generally weren't open to the public.

"Maybe Pea could say she has to research her family history?" Lou Lou suggested. "It wouldn't really be a lie."

Pea frowned. "I doubt anyone would let me do that without an adult. And what if that adult is Vice-Mayor Argyle?"

"Get a ladder and crawl in through a window?" Jeremy offered.

"That sounds dangerous," Lou Lou answered. "And illegal."

"Ask politely?" Pea said.

"I don't think that will work," Jeremy replied. "Particularly if we have to ask the vice-mayor."

Jeremy scratched his head, Pea looked out the window, lost in thought, and Lou Lou drummed her fingers on the kitchen counter as she considered their dilemma.

"I can't think of a good way," Lou Lou finally said. "Maybe this won't work."

"Eh hah e ke," Kyle said. Everyone turned to look at him. He was talking with his mouth full, having finished the beef bouillon caracol and moved on to the habanero one.

"Huh?" Jeremy said.

"Eh hah e ke," Kyle said again.

"We can't understand you, Kyle," Lou Lou said.

Kyle chewed and swallowed. "I have a key," he said.

"You have a what?" Pea asked.

"A key," said Kyle. "Since my dad works at City Hall, I volunteer there sometimes. Mostly I handle security and stop alien invasions from the planet Tyros with my supersonic lasers. But during the rare times when the aliens are quiet, I do filing in the City Archives. So they gave me a key."

Lou Lou's, Pea's, and Jeremy's jaws all dropped.

"Jeepers, Kyle! Why didn't you tell us this in the first place?" Lou Lou said.

"Because you never asked, Lou Lou Bombay," Kyle replied.

CHAPTER THIRTEEN
Operation Diary Mission Interplanetary 12 with Universe Coordinates 30/50

Once Kyle told Lou Lou, Pea, and Jeremy that he had a key to the City Archives, they made a plan to actually go there. Kyle insisted on calling this plan Operation Diary Mission Interplanetary 12 with Universe Coordinates 30/50. Since he had the key, nobody disagreed with him, but Lou Lou and Pea called it the Diary Mission for short.

The Diary Mission was scheduled for Thursday after school, which felt to Lou Lou like an eternity away. She tried to focus on schoolwork and her new crop of hyacinths in her garden, but all she could think about was Thursday. Lou Lou even forgot Wednesday was her half birthday until her dad surprised her with half of a capsize cake.

"Thanks!" Lou Lou said after her parents sang half of "Happy Birthday." She pulled the top half of a candle out of the sunken-in middle of the cake and licked off the gooey chocolate, then gobbled down her piece. She'd meant to only eat half, but Lou Lou couldn't resist capsize cake. "May I be excused now so I can call Pea?"

"Sure," her dad said. "But don't be long because we're going to watch *Survival at Sea*. Tonight we'll find out who gets voted off the ship."

"¡Feliz medio cumpleaños!" Pea said when she answered Lou Lou's call. "There's not really a perfect translation for 'half birthday' so I had to make something up."

"Gracias!" Lou Lou replied. "We're still on for tomorrow, right? I can't wait to get the diary and take back the Bonanza!"

"Yes, but we shouldn't get our hopes up too high," Pea replied. "It's possible that we won't find anything in the diary that proves it's a fake." Lou Lou knew that this was true. Even though they had a plan, it might not go . . . according to plan.

"I suppose we should think positively about it," Pea

added. "As Diane von Furstenberg said, 'Attitude is everything!'" Lou Lou agreed.

Pea changed the subject. "I visited Abuela Josie tonight, and she told me something interesting. My tío Diego was a wonderful baker, and he came up with our city's recipe for caracoles!"

"Wow! Does Abuela Josie know the secret ingredient?"

"Por desgracia, no," Pea replied.

"Bummer!" said Lou Lou. "I guess Jeremy will have to keep experimenting with the recipe."

"Maybe we won't be taste testers next time, though," Pea said. Lou Lou laughed.

"Lou Lou!" her dad called from the living room. "The show is on! I think Sailor Sue might walk the plank!"

"Gotta go," Lou Lou said.

"¡Hasta mañana!" Pea replied.

· ›› • ‹‹ ·

Lou Lou could barely sit still in her classes the next day as she thought about the Diary Mission. It didn't help that every time she glanced at Kyle he winked like they shared a secret. Which they did, of course, but Kyle's wink was so exaggerated—pulling down the bottom half of his forehead and pushing up the top half of his cheek—that other people noticed. In Science, after his tenth wink of the day, Danielle Desserts finally said, "Why does Kyle keep doing that? Is he your new boyfriend, Lou Lou?"

"No way," Lou Lou grumbled down at her desk.

Finally, the end of the school day arrived and Lou Lou, Kyle, and Jeremy headed off toward City Hall.

"Is that really necessary?" Lou Lou asked Kyle as he put on his silver Comet Cop cape. "It makes us stand out, and we're trying to keep this thing under the radar."

"It's absolutely necessary, Lou Lou Bombay. No Comet Cop mission is complete without a cape, and that includes Operation Diary Mission Interplanetary 12 with Universe Coordinates 30/50." Lou Lou knew it was useless to argue with Kyle about anything Comet Cop–related, so she let it go.

City Hall was in the Centro Circle neighborhood, but still walking distance from El Corazón Public. On the way, Lou Lou told Jeremy about Diego creating the recipe for caracoles. All the while, Kyle chattered on about how he wasn't *really* breaking any rules by going into the City Archives, but, even if he was bending them slightly, it was all in the interest of rescuing the Bonanza

and the space goats and helping Peacock . . . Earthlings, that is.

When City Hall came into view, Lou Lou marveled at the building even though she'd seen it countless times before. City Hall towered over the plaza below and looked to Lou Lou like a sparkling magic castle. It had a beautiful arched entryway that led to a ballroom-size hall topped by a large dome. On each end of the building was a tower and two turrets, and from one tower flew a city flag showing a fox and a bear shaking hands flanked by a grand bridge. On the front of the building was written the city's motto: *AMIGA DE TODOS*. Lou Lou wasn't sure what was inside the towers and turrets, but she'd always imagined it was dragons or a princess with impossibly long hair.

Pea was waiting on a bench in front when they arrived. She stood up to give Lou Lou a hug and greet Kyle and Jeremy.

"Helllooo!" Lou Lou said in a singsong voice. Her ears tingled. "Ready?"

"Roger that!" Kyle said into an imaginary headset. "Operation Diary Mission Interplanetary 12 with Universe Coordinates 30/50 has a green light!"

"I guess that means we should go inside now?" Pea's

voice wavered, and Lou Lou knew Pea was nervous. Lou Lou had to admit that she was, too, but she was even more excited.

"¡Vámonos!" said Jeremy.

"Let's go rescue our Bonanza!" Lou Lou said, and into City Hall they went.

CHAPTER FOURTEEN
Gazebo Enthusiast

Kyle led the way into City Hall's marble foyer, which was lined with busts of past mayors and statues of Diego and Giles. It was bustling with people, and Lou Lou and Pea nearly bumped into a bride and groom posing for a photograph.

"Perdón," Pea said, then added, "¡Felicidades!"

Lou Lou, Pea, and Jeremy followed Kyle up a staircase to a long hallway. As they walked, they passed Mayor Montoya's dark office and Lou Lou thought about poor Putt Putt the puli.

"We have arrived, Earthlings!" Kyle said when they

reached a door marked CITY ARCHIVES/ARCHIVOS DE LA CIUDAD.

"Quick, open it and let's go in before someone sees us," Lou Lou said. Kyle unzipped his backpack and took out a giant key ring holding at least fifteen keys.

"Yowza! What do you need all those for?" Jeremy asked.

"To unlock the mysteries of the universe, of course," replied Kyle. "Also one is for my house, one is for my auntie's house, one is for my sister's room—but don't tell her I have it—one is for—"

"Okay, okay. Just let us in," Lou Lou interrupted.

"I always forget which key it is," Kyle said. Lou Lou stamped her foot impatiently. "I'll just have to try a few." As Kyle tested the keys in the lock, Lou Lou noticed that the door on her left said VICE-MAYOR'S OFFICE. It was slightly ajar, so she could see that the office was empty.

"Pea!" She nudged her best friend. "That's Andy Argyle's office! I'm going to take a quick peek." Before Pea could answer, Lou Lou ducked inside. Lou Lou's nerves felt jumpy—it wouldn't be good to get caught snooping around the vice-mayor's office. But what if there was a clue that Andy Argyle was hiding? Lou Lou had to have a look just in case.

The vice-mayor's office was furnished with a large wooden desk, bookshelves, and two chairs. A black-and-white argyle jacket hung from a coatrack in the corner above two pairs of Andy Argyle's shiny shoes. On the wall near the desk was a photograph of Amanda smirking in front of a gazebo by a river. To its left was another photo of her father in a gazebo in a field, and a third of the Argyles together in a gazebo in front of a grand house.

Lou Lou walked over to the desk. The surface was bare except for ten or more miniature gazebos, each one different. How strange, thought Lou Lou. She moved on to the bookcase, which held a row of issues of the same magazine, *Gazebo Enthusiast*. The vice-mayor sure does like gazebos, she thought.

On the upper shelf of the bookcase was a small gazebo statue, a book called *The Top Ten Gazebos of the*

World, and gazebo bookends. Lou Lou stood on her tip-toes to see the top of the bookcase and caught a glimpse of the ceiling. The entire thing was painted to look like the dome of a fancy gazebo.

"Wow!" Lou Lou said. Even though she didn't like Andy Argyle, she couldn't help but be impressed. Then Lou Lou heard Pea call her name.

"Lou Lou! Kyle opened the door! Hurry!" Lou Lou scampered back to join her friends. Kyle and Jeremy were already inside the City Archives, but Pea was waiting at the door.

"Find anything?" Pea asked.

"Nothing related to the diary," Lou Lou replied. "But a lot of gazebo stuff. I'll tell you more about it later. Let's go in!"

Pea hesitated. They were about to break the rules by going into the City Archives, and Pea wasn't a fan of rule-breaking. Lou Lou could understand, but the importance of looking for the diary was greater than other concerns.

"Don't worry," said Lou Lou. "Just think of how nice it will be to get the Bonanza and your hats back." Pea took a deep breath, nodded, and followed Lou Lou through the door.

Once they were all inside, Kyle flipped on the light and dimmed it to the lowest setting.

"Shouldn't we keep it off?" Pea asked nervously.

"No one will notice it if we shut the door," Jeremy said, pulling the heavy door closed behind them.

The City Archives was a medium-size room that looked like a mix of Abuela Josie's attic, a library, a museum, and an office. There were stacks of dusty books, overstuffed filing cabinets, and photographs on the walls. Lou Lou glanced at a row of photos from previous Bonanzas, each of which was labeled with the city's age and the name of the host neighborhood. At the end of the row was a blank spot and a label that said, *Two Hundred Years, El Corazón*. It made Lou Lou's ears burn to see that someone had crossed out *El Corazón* and scrawled *Verde Valley* underneath. Lou Lou had nothing against Verde Valley, but the Bonanza situation felt so unfair to her own neighborhood.

Lou Lou stood beside Pea and looked at the images from past celebrations. Some showed caracoles, some were crowd scenes, and others were photos of various performances. Pea gazed longingly at photographs of fancy hats, including one of a girl surrounded by hatboxes, captioned *Marta Oro, Milliner's Apprentice, 1928*.

"We'd best start looking for the diary so we can get *your* hats back, Pea," Lou Lou said.

Lou Lou and Pea went to help Jeremy and Kyle sort through a pile of books. But first, Pea noticed a glass display case in one corner half-hidden by a large box.

"I think I see Giles's actual jaunty cap!" Pea went to have a look. "The fabric has worn so well for being—" She stopped in mid-sentence and crouched down to peer at a lower shelf in the case. "I found it!" she said, careful to keep her exclamation to a whisper. "I found the diary!"

Lou Lou, Kyle, and Jeremy rushed over. Sure enough, there was the small book on the same shelf as a letter opener engraved with the initials *GW*.

"Wow! Great job, Pea!" said Lou Lou. "Now let's take a look before someone notices that we're here!" Lou Lou tugged at the handle of the display case, but it didn't open. She changed her grip and tugged again.

"Hmm," she said when it still didn't budge. She was reminded of a time not so long ago when she and Pea were trying to open a door in the candle shop. All it took was some muscle and determination—surely the same was true here. She gave the handle a harder pull. No movement. "Arrr!" she said like one of her dad's movie pirates.

"Do you think it's locked?" asked Pea.

"There's no place for a key. It's just stuck," replied Lou Lou.

"Move aside, por favor!" said Jeremy. "I'll open it for you. Piece of cake." Jeremy gave it his best pull, but the door didn't open for him either.

"Piece of cake, huh?" said Lou Lou.

"Dun dun dun!" From behind Lou Lou, Pea, and Jeremy came a noise indicating that they should be impressed. "Comet Cop to the rescue!" Kyle cried. "I'll open the door with my invisible super-strength multipurpose space tool!" Kyle pulled something from his bag.

"That's a regular old screwdriver, Kyle," Lou Lou said.

"And we can see it, so it's not invisible," Pea pointed out.

Kyle ignored them and stuck the screwdriver into the little space under the display door. He pried it open with a *pop!*

"Told you it was multipurpose!" he said.

"I don't think we can argue with that," said Jeremy. "Job well done, Kyle." Kyle beamed and looked at Pea. She smiled.

"Yes, buen trabajo!" Pea said.

Lou Lou picked up the diary from inside the display case and flipped through it. The pages weren't blank, but luckily the diary wasn't very long, so it wouldn't take too much time to read. Lou Lou was going to suggest she skim through and read passages aloud while the others listened for clues that it was a fake.

But then they heard the door creak open.

CHAPTER FIFTEEN
Accidentally Borrowed

"Hide!" said Jeremy as the City Archives door slowly opened. Lou Lou, Pea, Jeremy, and Kyle dove behind a large trunk. Lou Lou tucked the diary into her satchel. Jeremy reached up and pushed down his hair's red spikes so they couldn't be seen.

"Is it Vice-Mayor Argyle?" whispered Pea, her voice trembling.

"I don't know. But if it is and he finds us, we're in so much trouble," Kyle replied. "I'm technically not supposed to bring any unauthorized persons or space aliens in here."

No one said a word as they heard the door open wider. Lou Lou rubbed her ears to ease the burning. Pea was frozen in place. Kyle bit his pinkie fingernail, and Jeremy rolled a piece of his hair around in his fingers.

"Hello? Who's in here?" a woman called. Lou Lou exhaled quietly and her ears cooled a little. At least it wasn't the vice-mayor. All of a sudden, her nose began to tickle. *Oh no,* Lou Lou thought. *Please not now.* But she couldn't help it.

"Achoo!" sneezed Lou Lou. Pea's eyes went even wider.

"I know there is *someone* in here," the woman's voice said. "I heard you! Come out at once!"

This is it. We're busted, thought Lou Lou. Then Kyle put a *keep quiet* finger to his lips and made an *okay* sign with his other hand. He stood up. "Greetings, Wanda," Kyle said.

"Kyle? What are you doing here? You don't volunteer on Thursdays."

"Not usually," Kyle replied. "But I came in today to finish some filing. It's important to have everything in perfect planetary order before the Bonanza!"

"Oh my, you really are a lovely boy," Wanda said. "Albeit a little odd." Lou Lou didn't have to look to know that the woman was eyeing Kyle's cape.

"Well, I'm done here for today," Kyle said. "Wanda, have I ever showed you my cosmic kung fu?"

"I don't believe you have," Wanda replied. "But I'm not sure—"

"You've really got to see it," said Kyle. "I will teach you a shooting-star side kick so you can defend yourself in case of an invasion from the Tyrosians. But we need to go outside to the courtyard so we have more space."

Lou Lou peeked over the trunk just in time to see Kyle gently pulling on the arm of a woman in a blue dress with big blond hair. Wanda didn't see Lou Lou, but Kyle looked at her and raised his eyebrows as if to say, *Make a break for it, Lou Lou Bombay*. Once Kyle and Wanda's voices disappeared down the hall, that's exactly what Lou Lou, Pea, and Jeremy did, rushing out of the City Archives, down the hall and the stairs, through the grand foyer, down the front steps, and into the spring sun. When they were a safe distance from City Hall, they stopped to catch their breath and calm their nerves.

"Lou Lou!" Pea said between huffs and puffs. "I can't believe we stole the diary."

"We didn't really *steal* it," Lou Lou replied. "We accidentally borrowed it."

"She's got a point," Jeremy said.

"We better give it back before anyone notices. We could get in big trouble," said Pea.

"She's got a point, too," Jeremy said.

"Don't worry. We'll return it," replied Lou Lou. "But now that we have it—accidentally, of course—we might as well read it to see if we can get the Bonanza back!"

"That's the best point of all!" Jeremy said.

· >> • << ·

After their close-call Diary Mission, Lou Lou, Pea, and Jeremy didn't have enough time to examine the diary before they were all due home. Pea said she'd hold on to it until they could get together again to read it.

The following morning, Lou Lou saw Kyle in English class. She never thought she'd be so grateful to him. He'd helped Lou Lou and Pea once before to solve a mystery without knowing he was doing it. But this time, Kyle had been genuinely brave, and he was the reason that they weren't all in big trouble right now.

Lou Lou stopped at Kyle's desk on the way to hers. "Thanks for what you did yesterday," she said. Lou Lou noticed Danielle staring at her. Kyle saw it, too.

"I don't know what you're talking about, Lou Lou

Bombay!" he said loudly. "Perhaps the gravitational forces on this planet have affected your brain." Then, under his breath he said, "Bring it back to me as soon as you can."

"I knew it! I knew you had a crush on him! Or he has a crush on you! Or whatever!" Danielle said. Lou Lou just rolled her eyes and moved on to her desk.

After school, Lou Lou and Pea met as usual at the SS *Lucky Alley* for PSPP tea and scones. Jeremy couldn't join them because he had Comic Book Club, which also ruled out Kyle coming over. Today, the girls only managed formal PSPP hellos before abandoning polite speech and moving on to diary talk.

"Where should we start?" Lou Lou asked, turning the diary around in her hands. "Have you read any of it yet?"

"I copied a few pages to practice my penmanship, but I was waiting for you to do the serious reading," Pea said.

"Great!" Lou Lou skimmed through the diary until she found the entry that Andy Argyle had read at the Heliotrope. She was a little disappointed that it said exactly what he'd said it did about the Bonanza and Verde Valley. But as Pea pointed out, if the vice-mayor had faked what he read from the diary, he would definitely make sure the actual diary backed up his story.

Next, Lou Lou opened to a random page and began to read aloud:

"Date: The twelfth of April.

Dearest Diary,

Diego and I are truly happy in our lovely new home, Verde Valley. Together we have built a beautiful gazebo like the one in Barnaby-on-Pudding, but our gazebo is painted in the style of Diego's village. We hope that Verde Valley and the surrounding land will become a grand city! More settlers will join us here soon, including my darling, Alice. The climate is ideal for her pet goats."

Lou Lou paused. "Pet goats? That's not true, right? Giles's wife didn't have pet goats, so the diary is not real!"

Pea shook her head. "Actually, that part is definitely true. That's one reason Kyle was training goats for the Bonanza, remember?"

"Oh, yeah." Lou Lou had forgotten that Kyle's landscaping "space" goats also had some historical meaning. She skipped ahead to another page.

"Date: The thirtieth of April.

Dearest Diary,

O happy day! Alice has finally come to Verde Valley. Diego's paramour, Catalina, is here as well. To celebrate their arrival, we had a picnic

in our beautiful gazebo. Alice left her goats at
home so they wouldn't get sunburned, but I think
she enjoyed herself nonetheless."

"Argh, I don't want to hear any more about the stupid goats!" Lou Lou thought back to the first passage Pea had read. The part about the gazebo reminded Lou Lou of something. "Pea, with all the Diary Mission excitement I never told you about Andy Argyle's office. It was filled with gazebo paraphernalia! There were photos, miniatures, and even magazines called *Gazebo Exorcist!*" Pea looked confused. "I mean *Gazebo Enthusiast!*" Lou Lou said. "And the whole ceiling was painted to look like a gazebo dome."

"Interesting!" Pea replied. "I guess that means Vice-Mayor Argyle will be excited to have the new gazebo in Verde Valley. But it doesn't really prove anything, except that he likes gazebos."

"Right." Lou Lou flipped through the pages of the diary. "There's got to be something in here that's useful!" She was getting frustrated.

"Maybe we should start reading from the beginning?" Pea suggested gently.

"Sure, the beginning seems like a good place to . . . begin." Lou Lou opened to the first page and read aloud from the diary while Pea nibbled on a raspberry scone. It started with Giles's tale of his sea journey from Barnaby-on-Pudding. The talk of great sailing ships and storms was the sort of thing that Lou Lou's dad would like, but it wasn't helpful to Lou Lou and Pea. Lou Lou took a bite of her own scone and skipped ahead until she found the entry from Giles's arrival:

"Date: The second of March.
Dearest Diary,
I have some wonderful news to share. Today, I finally arrived in this new land and also made a friend! He is a man from the south named Diego who is just as eager as I am to make this lovely place a home. I do not speak his language, nor he mine, but I am confident we will learn. He seems very kind. Oh, and he has a beautiful chestnut mare! The weather here—"

"Wait! I just remembered something!" Pea said. She almost never interrupted Lou Lou, so Lou Lou knew it had to be important.

"Really? Something helpful?" Lou Lou asked. She hoped Pea's great memory would save the day.

"Chestnut. You said 'chestnut mare,'" Pea replied.

"Yes. So . . . ?"

Pea's blue eyes lit up in a way that made her whole face glow. "Abuela Josie told us that Diego's horse was—"

"Sorrel!" It was Lou Lou's turn to interrupt Pea. "You're a genius! We got it, Pea! The diary is wrong about the color of Diego's horse, so it must be a fake. I knew it all along!" Lou Lou closed the small book with a triumphant clap. They were sure to get the Bonanza back now! She could hardly believe it had been so easy!

CHAPTER SIXTEEN
Chestnut

"What do we do next?" asked Pea after they discovered the chestnut mistake. "Should we keep reading?"

"No need!" replied Lou Lou. "This is proof that the Argyles faked the diary! Now we have to tell someone who can help."

"Our parents? Abuela Josie?" Pea said.

"No, I think it should be someone not related to us. So they don't look biased when we all make the announcement that saves the Bonanza for El Corazón." Lou Lou was already thinking ahead to the ultimate victory.

Pea took a sip of tea. "How about Principal Garcia?"

She was referring to the principal of El Corazón Public. "He's a good listener and people respect him, even outside of our neighborhood."

"That's a great idea, Pea!" Lou Lou replied. "We should go see him tomorrow."

"But tomorrow is Saturday," said Pea. "Surely, he won't be in his office."

"¡No es problemo!" Lou Lou said.

"Problema," Pea corrected gently.

"¡No es problema! I know where he lives. He had my English class over to his house last year for homemade horchata after we won the school reading challenge. He told us that his door is always open to students. So really he invited us to drop by anytime!"

"I'm not sure that's exactly what he meant. But it's worth a try," replied Pea.

"Let's meet here in the morning and walk to his house. It's so exciting, Pea! We'll get this sorted out and take back the Bonanza and your hats!" She stood on her chair. "Like I said before, Lou Lou and Pea to—whoa!—whoa!" The chair wobbled and Lou Lou slipped off and fell onto the grass.

"Oh no!" Pea dropped her scone on the table. "Are you okay?"

Lou Lou got up and grinned. "I'm fine! Now, where was I? Oh, I know—Lou Lou and Pea to the rescue again!"

· ›› ∗ ‹‹ ·

At ten on Saturday morning, Lou Lou and Pea went off to see Principal Garcia. Lou Lou brought a bag of her dad's spinnaker-pole cinnamon rolls to munch on while they walked. She was awake and alert, and had already spent two hours in her sunny garden.

Pea, on the other hand, was sleepy-eyed and yawning. She clutched her blue tote bag, which held the diary, and shook her head to clear the just-woke-up fogginess.

"It would have been polite to bring something for Principal Garcia," Pea said.

"How about the rest of the spinnaker-pole cinnamon rolls?" Lou Lou suggested. She peered into the paper bag. There were only two left, and she'd already broken a piece off one to eat it. When Pea looked away, Lou Lou stuck the piece back on. With the gooey icing, Principal Garcia would never notice.

Lou Lou and Pea arrived at Principal Garcia's house, a Victorian-style home painted sea-foam green and turquoise. Pea paused as they reached the flagstones leading to the front steps.

"Lou Lou, what if we get in trouble for accidentally borrowing the diary?"

"That won't happen," replied Lou Lou. "Principal Garcia will be happy we told him about the fake diary, and once the Argyles are exposed, no one will care that we accidentally borrowed it. El Corazón will get the Bonanza back and we'll be heroines!"

"Okay," said Pea, though she still sounded hesitant.

"And we'll get your hats, too!" said Lou Lou. She was already marching up the principal's steps, so Pea didn't have time for more doubts.

Lou Lou rang the doorbell and Principal Garcia appeared, wearing a white tank top, paisley-print shorts, and rainbow socks. Lou Lou suppressed a giggle at the principal's weekend attire.

"Why hello, Lou Lou and Peacock. What are you girls doing here?" asked Principal Garcia. He smiled under his bushy mustache, but he was clearly surprised by their visit.

"We have something very important to tell you!" Lou Lou blurted out.

"I already took your advice about planting both shrubs

and flowers in my backyard," said Principal Garcia.

Lou Lou was impressed. "Mixing greenery with bright blooms creates an eye-catching effect."  She remembered the purpose of their trip and said again, "We have something very important to tell you!"

Pea looked at Lou Lou out of the corner of her eye and took over the conversation. "May we please have a chat, Principal Garcia? We brought spinnaker-pole cinnamon rolls."

Lou Lou held up the paper bag.

"Of course, come in," Principal Garcia replied. "I'm not sure what a spinnaker pole has to do with a cinnamon roll, but I've never met a breakfast pastry I didn't like."

"Me neither!" said Lou Lou. "Actually, I'm not crazy about cheese danishes." Principal Garcia laughed and held the door open.

Lou Lou and Pea followed Principal Garcia into his

kitchen, where they sat at the table with glasses of home-made horchata. He listened intently as Lou Lou and Pea explained that Diego's horse was actually sorrel, not chestnut, and that this proved that Giles's diary was a fake. When Lou Lou asked when they could get the Bonanza back for El Corazón, Principal Garcia held up his hands.

"Hold your horses!" he said, and chuckled. Lou Lou and Pea smiled politely. Principal Garcia's face turned serious. "Joking aside, this is a big accusation, niñas. Before we can talk about reclaiming the Bonanza, I need to call the vice-mayor so we can all discuss this diary issue." He picked up the phone book from a side table and scanned through it.

Pea looked a little nervous, but Lou Lou said, "Sure!" She was interested to see what the Argyles had to say for themselves. Would they apologize? Offer right then and there to return Pea's hats and the rest of El Corazón's Bonanza crafts and preparations? Run away ashamed?

Principal Garcia called the vice-mayor and repeated the diary story. Pea raised her eyebrows at Lou Lou.

Don't worry, Lou Lou mouthed.

"The Argyles are coming over to talk this through,"

Principal Garcia said when he hung up. Pea clenched her fists under the table. Lou Lou reached over and squeezed her hand.

It wasn't long before they heard the screech of tires outside followed by the doorbell.

"Let yourselves in, por favor!" Principal Garcia called. The door slammed and feet stomped down the hall. Amanda's angry red face appeared in the kitchen doorway, and Lou Lou knew right then that El Corazón wasn't going to get the Bonanza back without a fight.

CHAPTER SEVENTEEN
Big Trouble

"Gimme!" Amanda stuck out her hand, palm up, at Lou Lou and Pea. She flipped one of her braids over her shoulder.

"Hello, Amanda," said Principal Garcia. "Please sit down and have some horchata."

"We're not here for horchata. We just want to reclaim what is rightfully ours." The vice-mayor's voice boomed from around the corner before his dark eyes appeared.

"He means Giles's diary!" added Amanda, even though everyone knew that. "Which is SO not a fake. And it belongs to us!"

"Doesn't it belong to our city?" Pea asked.

"Quick thinking," Lou Lou whispered.

"That's true," said Principal Garcia.

"Even so, you can't just *steal* it from the City Archives," Andy said.

"Also true," said Principal Garcia.

"We didn't *steal* it!" said Lou Lou. "We just accidentally *borrow*—"

"Whatever!" screeched Amanda. "Just give it back!" Principal Garcia nodded to Pea, and she took the diary from her bag and handed it to Amanda. Amanda stuffed it into her red-and-pink-argyle-print backpack.

"It doesn't matter who has the diary. What matters is that we can prove it's fake and you're using it to take the Bonanza away from El Corazón," Lou Lou said.

Andy Argyle let out a sinister laugh. Principal Garcia's kitchen didn't have the acoustics of the Heliotrope but the *Ha! Ha! Ha!* still seemed to echo all around them. "Ah yes, your ridiculous accusation based on the color of Diego's horse," he said. "Let's dispense with that now. Amanda, tell them."

Amanda smirked and pulled from her bag a book with the title *Equine Rainbow*. She opened to a marked page and read aloud: "'*Chestnut*' and '*sorrel*' are often used *interchangeably in the equine world to describe a horse with a red-hued coat. 'Chestnut' has English origins, whereas 'sorrel' is Western.* And there you have it!" Amanda slammed the book closed.

"What my darling daughter says is true. Chestnut and sorrel are the same color. So there is no error in the so-called fake diary." Andy Argyle made air quotes around the word *fake.*

"It seems that one horse's sorrel is another horse's chestnut, niñas," said Principal Garcia to Lou Lou and Pea. "And it's not surprising that Giles used the English term in his diary. He was from England after all." His voice softened. "I know you're disappointed about the Bonanza—believe me, I am, too—but there is no proof that the diary is not one hundred percent real."

Lou Lou didn't know what to say. Her ears were burning, but as much as she disliked and distrusted the Argyles, she couldn't disagree. She glanced at Pea, who was wide-eyed and now had her hands clasped tightly in front of her on the table.

"I trust that clears this up," said the vice-mayor to Principal Garcia. He turned his dark eyes toward Lou Lou and Pea. "Amanda and I don't appreciate being called liars. And I really don't appreciate your thievery!

How exactly did you steal the diary from the City Archives?"

"We didn't steal, we *borrow*—"

"They probably had help from their friends!" Amanda cut Lou Lou off. Her tone was mean, but Lou Lou also detected a hint of jealousy.

"Perhaps you had assistance on the inside," Andy Argyle said. "Tell me how you did it!"

Lou Lou racked her brains for an answer that wouldn't cast suspicion on Kyle.

"My History of Art class went to the City Archives to look at photographs of early murals," Pea said. Pea obviously didn't want to tell on Kyle either.

"I see! So you pilfered the diary then!" replied Andy Argyle. Lou Lou wasn't sure what *pilfered* meant, but she knew it couldn't be good.

Pea was quiet. She had managed to save Kyle without really lying since she truly had once gone to the City Archives with her class. *Brilliant!* thought Lou Lou, until she realized that now Pea was going to get in trouble.

"I—" Lou Lou started to say, but Pea kicked her lightly under the table. Clearly, she knew Lou Lou was also about to claim responsibility, but Pea was the best of best friends and was trying to keep Lou Lou out of trouble.

"You'll have to be disciplined for this," Andy Argyle said to Pea. "And you, too." He looked at Lou Lou. "Even if *you* didn't actually participate in the theft, you're still part of this plot to undermine us! Wouldn't you agree, Principal Garcia?"

"Now, now," said Principal Garcia. "Maybe we can just let this go, Vice-Mayor Argyle. You have the diary back, and the girls only thought they were doing the right—" Just then, Pea's phone rang. She'd placed it on the table when she'd retrieved the diary. The caller came up as *Mamá*. Before Pea could answer, Andy Argyle snatched the phone.

"No, wait!" said Lou Lou. But it was too late.

"Hello, this is Andy Argyle, vice-mayor and Bicen-

tennial Bonanza Boss, speaking." He sneered at Lou Lou and Pea.

"Ha! You're in big trouble now!" cackled Amanda. Lou Lou's hands were cold from the horchata glass, so she used them to cool her fiery ears.

"I'm afraid we've got a big problem," the vice-mayor said into the phone. "Did you know that your daughter and her friend are diary thieves?"

As Andy Argyle explained what he thought had happened, Lou Lou looked over at Pea. She had her head in her hands. Lou Lou felt terrible. She was still certain something fishy was up with the Argyles. But none of this would have happened if she hadn't been so eager to borrow the diary and so hasty in telling Principal Garcia about Diego's horse.

"Your mother would like to speak to you, Peacock. And she doesn't sound very pleased." Andy Argyle handed Pea her phone. Amanda giggled. "Let's go, Amanda, darling," the vice-mayor said. "We have what we came for." He turned and walked out of the kitchen.

"I told you! Big trouble!" Amanda gloated, pointing a skinny finger at Lou

Lou and Pea. She spun around, nearly hitting Lou Lou in the face with one of her long braids.

"Lo siento, lo siento, Mamá," Pea was saying into the phone. As much as Lou Lou hated to admit it, Amanda was right. They were definitely in big trouble now.

CHAPTER EIGHTEEN
Pea's News

When they arrived back at the SS *Lucky Alley*, Henry Pearl was already waiting to take Pea home. Before she got into her father's car, Pea looked grimly at Lou Lou.

"I don't think we can say our *See you tomorrow*s because I have a feeling that I'm grounded as of twenty minutes ago," she said.

"I'm so sorry, Pea," replied Lou Lou.

"It's not your fault." Pea pulled a huge glittery blue barrette from her bag and pinned it on the side of her head. She handed a similar red barrette to Lou Lou. "Elsa Schiaparelli said, 'In difficult times, fashion is always outrageous,'" Pea explained.

From the car, Pea's father called, "Peacock Paloma Pearl! Time to go now!"

"Buena suerte," Lou Lou said.

"You too." Pea nodded in the direction of Lou Lou's front steps, and Lou Lou turned to see her mom, cross-armed and frowning.

Lou Lou had thought maybe the Pearls wouldn't report her, but she knew it was unlikely. Parents were often similar to best friends in that they told each other everything.

It was no surprise that Lou Lou also ended up grounded for a week. Her mom called her Louise, a sure sign that she was really mad, and her dad said that Lou Lou's actions were not those of an honorable sailor and violated the SS *Lucky Alley* code of conduct. Lou Lou tried to explain their good intentions—that they wanted to reclaim the Bonanza and Pea's hats, and that they had only accidentally *borrowed* the diary—but her parents didn't want to hear "excuses."

The next few days, Lou Lou was on her best behavior. She helped her dad perfect his monkey's-fist nautical knot, darned a hole in her mom's fuzzy bathrobe, and worked hard on her homework. But she couldn't stop thinking about the Bonanza and all that El Corazón had lost. So Lou Lou was left moping around the crow's nest.

To make matters worse, on Wednesday, Andy Argyle came to pick up the model of the gazebo from Lou Lou's school. Lou Lou and her classmates watched their teacher, Mr. Anthem, unlock the hallway trophy case for the vice-mayor.

"We're certainly sorry to see this go. Everyone was really looking forward to the beautiful new Limonero Park gazebo," Mr. Anthem said.

"We were going to hold kazoo concerts in the gazebo on sunny days," one of Lou Lou's classmates said.

"And I was planning to use it for my pink princess birthday party, just like Sherry's party in the third Sugar Mountain Sisters book," said Danielle's friend.

So much for PSPP tea and scones in the gazebo, Lou Lou thought mournfully.

"Where in Verde Valley do you plan to put the gazebo?" Mr. Anthem asked. "Maybe my students can use it occasionally?"

"Oh, I doubt that," Andy Argyle scoffed. "And it's not really any of your business where I put it!" His shiny shoes squeaked as he grabbed the model and walked away. Watching the back of Andy Argyle's yellow-and-green jacket go out the door, Lou Lou felt a wave of hopelessness. If the diary was a fake, she had no way to prove it now. And she couldn't think of another way to get back the Bonanza. Plus, if the diary *was* real—a possibility Lou Lou had to consider—Verde Valley did deserve the Bonanza and the gazebo.

·>>·<<·

On Thursday after school, Lou Lou walked to Limonero Park. Even though she was grounded, she had permission from her parents to water the honeysuckle. Lou Lou was finishing up when a voice called out, "Hiya, Lou Lou Bombay!"

Lou Lou turned and saw Jeremy walking toward her.

"Hi! What are you up to?" she asked.

"I came to see you. Peacock thought you might be at the park today."

"Pea? When did you talk to Pea? How is she doing?" Lou Lou felt a twinge of sadness. It had been almost a whole week since she'd talked to her best friend. This was the longest both she and Pea had been grounded. In fact, Lou Lou couldn't remember a time when Pea had ever been grounded.

"I ran into her at the bodega. She's fine," Jeremy said. "But"— he leaned in conspiratorially— "she says she has news for us. About the diary." He was whispering even though there was no one around to hear him.

Lou Lou felt her ears tingle with excitement. "What news?" she asked.

"I don't know the details," Jeremy said. "She wants to explain it in person on Saturday and suggested you, me, and Comet Cop Kyle meet her at Cupcake Cabana at ten-thirty."

"I don't know if . . . never mind, I'll find a way to be there." Lou Lou was technically grounded until the end of first dogwatch on Saturday, which was nautical-speak for six p.m. But she thought she could negotiate time off her sentence for good behavior, particularly since Pea was clearly only grounded through Friday night.

"Bueno! See ya Saturday," said Jeremy. He started to walk away but then turned back to Lou Lou. "Hey, thanks for not telling on me for the Diary Mission," he said. "Pretty cool of you, Lou Lou Bombay. Pretty cool. I do feel bad that you and Peacock got in trouble. I'll make it up to you with some killer caracoles once I get the recipe right."

"Still working on the caracoles, huh?" said Lou Lou.

"Yeah, Rosa sampled my latest batches. Apparently, turmeric, mustard, and tuna salad aren't the right ingredients either."

"I'm not surprised," said Lou Lou. Tuna salad caracoles sounded worse than beef bouillon caracoles. "Oh, and you're welcome."

"Maybe the Diary Mission wasn't such a great idea," Jeremy said.

"That depends on what Pea tells us on Saturday!" Lou Lou replied. "If she's found a way to use the diary to get back the Bonanza, being grounded will definitely be worth it!"

CHAPTER NINETEEN
Pastry History

On Friday evening, Lou Lou crossed her fingers and pitched the idea of shortening her punishment to her parents. She could barely wait another day to hear Pea's news, let alone two! She held her breath while she waited for their decision.

"You *have* been extraordinarily helpful this week, Lou Lou," said her mom. She nodded at Lou Lou's dad and Lou Lou exhaled. It was a good sign that her mom hadn't called her Louise.

"As of the end of morning watch tomorrow, you are no longer grounded," said her dad. Translated from nautical-speak, this meant that Lou Lou was free after eight a.m.

"Thank you!" Lou Lou hugged her parents.

With her parents' permission, Lou Lou headed to Cupcake Cabana the next morning. She left a few minutes early so she could see the finished Bonanza mural on the way. The artists had decided to complete the painting as planned, even though Verde Valley had taken over the celebration.

The Bonanza mural was huge, colorful, and richly detailed. In the painting, Limonero Park was crowded with smiling people, many of whom were wearing Pea's fancy hats. Skilled brushstrokes were used to show the park's lemon trees and Lou Lou's honeysuckle. Abuela Josie was performing her famous stunt and Ella Divine sang in the gazebo. As she gazed at the mural, Lou Lou sighed and felt a familiar twinge of sadness. She hoped Pea had some good news.

Lou Lou was the first to arrive at Cupcake Cabana, with Jeremy right behind her. The shop was crowded, but they found a table and sat down to eat their cupcakes— vanilla with buttercream frosting for Lou Lou and chocolate double fudge for Jeremy. After what seemed like five eternities, Kyle arrived, followed by Pea.

"I missed you so much!" Lou Lou hopped up from her chair. It felt like ten eternities since she'd seen Pea, even though it had only been a week.

"Me too!" Pea said, readjusting her cardigan after Lou Lou's hug.

"Now tell me—" Lou Lou stopped herself. The polite thing to do was to ask if Pea wanted a cupcake.

As often happened, Pea read Lou Lou's thoughts. "It's okay." Pea smiled. "I'll get one after." She sat down in the empty chair between Lou Lou and Jeremy. "Hola, Jeremy. Hi, Kyle," Pea said. "Thank you for coming."

"I'm so glad you asked—" Kyle started enthusiastically. But then he quickly changed to his Comet Cop voice: "I mean, you're welcome, Earthling. I had to make time in my busy cosmic crime–fighting schedule, but that's acceptable."

"No prob!" Jeremy said. He wiped a white spot off his black leather jacket with his finger and stuck it in his mouth. Pea crinkled her nose ever so slightly.

"Powdered sugar," explained Jeremy. "I was making Mexican wedding cookies this morning."

Pea pulled two sheets of paper from her bag. At the top of one, Lou Lou saw the words *Penmanship Practice*.

"What does that have to do with the Bonanza?" Lou Lou asked impatiently. "Sorry," she added when she realized she was being impolite again.

"Before we had to give the diary back to the Argyles, I copied a bit as penmanship practice, remember?" Pea said.

"Yes," said Lou Lou. So much had happened in the past week, she'd forgotten about this.

"When I looked back at my work, I realized something important." Pea placed the top sheet of paper in the middle of the table so that everyone could see. "Look here." She pointed to a paragraph and read aloud:

"Date: The second of May.
Dearest Diary,
Alice is settling into Verde Valley quite nicely.
She called our dwellings 'crude,' but I am sure she
meant it in a charming way. I pointed out that
we have many conveniences; we even built an
oven so Diego could bake his scrumptious caracoles,
a pastry he just created! Alice loved the
caracoles, and her goats quickly gobbled them
up! Diego said agave is the secret ingredient that
makes the caracoles so delicious."

Pea looked up expectantly.

"I don't get it. How does this help?" asked Lou Lou. "Wait, I know! The diary is clearly a fake because goats don't eat pastries!"

"No—" started Pea.

Kyle cleared his throat loudly. "I can tell you from

my extensive experience with my goat battalion that they will eat absolutely anything. That includes space helmets, limited edition comic books, and superhero underwear."

"I'm confused," said Jeremy. "I tried agave in my caracoles and it didn't work."

"I remembered you told us that in the candle shop," Pea said. "So—

"Agave is the wrong ingredient!" Lou Lou said. "The diary is a fake because it's wrong about the caracoles! This is exactly what we've been looking for!" In her excitement, Lou Lou was almost shouting. She realized that she was attracting attention from people at nearby tables. "This is exactly what we've been looking for," Lou Lou said in a much quieter voice. "El Corazón can finally take back the Bonanza!"

"It's a cosmic miracle!" added Kyle.

"Hey, guys," Jeremy said. "This is really great. And I don't mean to be a downer, but—" Lou Lou held her breath. She didn't like the *but*—. "We still don't know the actual secret ingredient. So won't the Argyles say the diary is right about the agave and I'm just a bad baker? Even though that's clearly untrue."

"I was worried about that, too," Pea replied. "But then

something extraordinary happened." Pea showed them the second sheet of paper she'd taken from her bag. It was worn and fraying at the edges, and the writing was faded. Lou Lou could make out most of the black-inked words, but they were in Spanish, so she wasn't sure what she was reading. At the top of the page was written *Mi Receta* followed by what appeared to be a list. Jeremy read aloud:

"Harina, azúcar, huevos, mantequilla . . ."

"Aren't those foods?" asked Lou Lou. She didn't recognize all the words, but she knew that *azúcar* meant sugar and *huevos* meant eggs.

Pea nodded. She was smiling, and her blue eyes sparkled.

"It's the recipe!" Jeremy said, looking up from the page. "For caracoles!"

"¡Exactamente!" said Pea. "The original recipe complete with the *actual* secret ingredient!"

Jeremy grinned from ear to ear. "Peacock Pearl," he said, "I do believe that you have saved the day!"

CHAPTER TWENTY
See You Soon, Gazebo!

"How on earth, Pea?" Lou Lou asked. She could hardly believe that Pea had the real caracoles recipe!

"I was feeling sad about the Bonanza and my hats, so I decided to hang the painting of Tío Diego above my bureau. I thought it might help me feel better," Pea said.

"Just like Abuela Josie suggested," Lou Lou remembered.

"Sí. When I was attaching hanging wire, I saw something sticking out of the back of the frame. I pulled it out and it was the recipe!" Pea explained.

"That's amazing! Your tío Diego helped in a totally unexpected way!" said Lou Lou.

Jeremy's hands were trembling with excitement as he continued reading the recipe. Lou Lou felt it, too. They were finally about to learn the secret ingredient for the caracoles and prove the diary was a fake. Everyone would know about the Argyles' trickery and El Corazón would get back the Bonanza, the gazebo, and Pea's hats, once and for all!

Jeremy's lips moved as he read the recipe. He nodded at each ingredient that he recognized. When his eyes scanned the end of the list, he shook one fist in the air in a victory salute.

"¡Madreselva!" Jeremy exclaimed.

"Huh?" Lou Lou asked. "Are you talking about my honeysuckle or about Puerta Madreselva, where Diego grew up?"

"Neither," said Jeremy. "Madreselva—honeysuckle—is the secret ingredient in caracoles!"

Jeremy turned the recipe toward Lou Lou and pointed at the paper. "See! It says it right there!" Sure enough, Lou Lou saw the words, *Nectár de madreselva* and guessed correctly that they meant honeysuckle nectar.

"That's what adds the special sweetness!" Lou Lou said.

Jeremy leaped up from his chair and grabbed Pea's hands. He gave her a twirl that ended in a hug and almost toppled a nearby table. Pea was smiling when Jeremy released her. She brushed a bit of Mexican wedding cookie powdered sugar from her sleeve. Then it was Lou Lou's turn to hug her best friend for the second time that morning.

"Incredible, Pea! Jeremy will win the caracoles contest. Your hats will come home! And we'll finally have PSPP in the gazebo. You're a heroine! A right clever lass!" Lou Lou used her dad's sailor praise.

"¡Gracias!" said Pea.

"I must add my cosmic compliments as well," said Kyle. He patted Pea awkwardly on the back. "I did think the habanero caracol was delicious, but I can't wait to try the real recipe. And I can share a caracol with Mercury now that I'll get my goats back!"

"I would be honored to have your space goats try my pastries, Kyle," said Jeremy. "Now I'm sorry to break up this party, but I've got some killer caracoles to make! May I copy the recipe, Peacock? I'd never forgive myself if the original fell victim to a baking accident!"

"Actually, I already did that for you." Pea pulled a third sheet of paper from her bag. Lou Lou was always amazed by how considerate Pea was.

"Thank you!" Jeremy stood up. "Hmm, I wonder where I could get some nectár de madreselva?" He grinned at Lou Lou.

"I suppose my honeysuckle could spare a bit of nectar," said Lou Lou, grinning back. She was happy she could play a role in saving the day.

"What are we waiting for then?" asked Jeremy. "Off we go!"

Before they went to Limonero Park, Lou Lou stopped at the SS *Lucky Alley* to grab seed jars for the nectar and check in with her parents. She wasn't going to risk getting grounded again. Twenty minutes later, Lou Lou, Jeremy, and Pea arrived at the park. Kyle had to go visit his auntie, but Pea promised they'd include him in any plan to expose the Argyles' lies.

The first bush in the long row of honeysuckle was in full bloom. The nectar of this variety was edible, so Lou Lou showed Jeremy and Pea how to extract it by picking a flower, pinching it, and pulling out the long white style in the flower's center.

"Make sure you only take nectar from the flowers, no berries, because most honeysuckle berries are poisonous," Lou Lou cautioned.

When they'd collected enough nectar, Jeremy rushed off to make his first batch of authentic caracoles with the promise that Lou Lou and Pea would be his taste testers.

After Jeremy left, Lou Lou and Pea went to the center of the park. The circle on the ground marking the planned spot for the gazebo was overgrown. Nobody had bothered to maintain it after the Bonanza and the gazebo left for Verde Valley. In the middle of the circle, somebody had stuck a sign into the earth that read: ¡ÁNIMO, EL CORAZÓN! TAL VEZ HEMOS PERDIDO EL GAZEBO PERO NO HEMOS PERDIDO NUESTRO CORAZÓN.

"Cheer up, El Corazon!" Pea translated. "We may have lost the gazebo, but we have not lost our heart."

"But now we know for sure that the Argyles lied! And we'll get the gazebo after all!" Lou Lou said triumphantly. "All thanks to you, Pea!"

Pea smiled. "What will our first Friday PSPP in the gazebo be like?" she asked.

"We'll eat caracoles," said Lou Lou. "They will go well with tea."

"We will have to wear something amazing," Pea chimed in. "As Edith Head said, 'You can have anything you want in life if you dress for it.'"

"And to quote Forest Buttercup, 'Potassium-based fertilizer is the best for fruit trees,'" Lou Lou said. "We'll have to wear your hats for PSPP, of course!" she added quickly, since her quote was a little off.

"I can't wait to get them back," said Pea, smiling. "Especially Abuela Josie's lucky hat. And the one I made for myself." Pea's expression suddenly changed to worry. "Lou Lou, will anyone even believe us about the diary after the chestnut-and-sorrel fiasco?"

"We'll figure out a way to make everyone believe!" said Lou Lou. "It shouldn't be hard. It's the truth after all! Let's go back to my house and plan."

"I like that idea," said Pea. She linked arms with Lou Lou.

"See you soon, gazebo!" Lou Lou said to the empty space in the park.

"¡Hasta pronto, gazebo!" Pea added, and the best friends happily strolled off toward the SS *Lucky Alley*.

CHAPTER TWENTY-ONE
Amanda Loves Cupcakes

Lou Lou and Pea decided their next step should be to tell Abuela Josie about the fake diary. Pea's abuela was sure to believe them now that they had proof, and with her on their side, everyone else would believe them, too! They'd visit Abuela Josie on Monday afternoon, but in the meantime, Pea said they should keep their discovery a secret. Lou Lou knew it would be hard for her not to share the exciting news with everyone, but she also knew Pea was right.

On Monday at school, Lou Lou smiled inside every time she heard someone talk about the Bonanza. When a boy in Math was sad because he couldn't perform his magic show at the celebration, Lou Lou said three *chrysanthemum*s so she wouldn't tell him not to ditch his rabbit-in-a-hat quite yet. And when she overheard a teacher lament that she couldn't throw her daughter's birthday party in the gazebo, Lou Lou quickly walked away.

Lou Lou had permission from her parents to go straight to Pea's house after school. She met her best friend on her front steps.

"Should we go straight to Abuela Josie's?" Lou Lou asked.

"No, come inside first. I have two things to show you!" Pea held the door open for Lou Lou.

When they entered Pea's kitchen, Lou Lou immediately spied a beautiful red vaquera hat on the table.

"You finished it!" she said, hurrying to get a closer look. The hat had turned out beautifully with the rhinestone-dotted brim, a shiny new silver chain, and a cluster of black-and-brown feathers on one side.

"Rooster," Pea explained when Lou Lou gently touched a feather. "They were a better fit on this hat than peacock."

"Abuela Josie is going to love it!" Lou Lou said. "It's exactly right for her."

"As Christian Dior said, a hat 'is very often the best way to show your personality.'"

"She'll have double the personality once we've taken back the Bonanza and her lucky hat is returned," said Lou Lou. "She can wear that one for her stunt and her new hat for the rest of the celebration."

"Yes!" Pea beamed. "I thought we'd give this to her today."

Lou Lou had been so distracted by the hat that it was only now she noticed a brown bag also on the table. From the butter stains on the paper, she guessed immediately what was inside.

"Jeremy's caracoles!"

Pea nodded. "He brought them over yesterday evening."

"How do they taste?" Lou Lou asked.

"I haven't tried one yet. I was waiting for you!"

Lou Lou couldn't believe Pea's patience. If Jeremy had brought the pastries to Lou Lou first, she definitely would have sampled them already.

Pea took out two caracoles and put them on little blue plates.

"Papá?" She reached for another plate when her father walked into the kitchen.

"No, thank you," said Henry Pearl. "I'm watching my

figure. It's almost swimsuit season." He patted his trim belly and Lou Lou giggled.

Lou Lou wasted no time biting into the caracol, and Pea did the same. They watched each other as they chewed.

"Wow! It's perfect!" said Lou Lou halfway through her first mouthful.

Pea finished chewing. "¡Increíble! They taste just like Señora Basa's! She'd be so impressed. She always said, 'No hay nada mejor que un caracol delicioso.'"

Lou Lou raised her eyebrows.

"There's nothing better than a delicious caracol," Pea translated.

"We should congratulate Jeremy," Lou Lou said. "He'll definitely win the caracoles contest now!"

"Let's call him later! But first let's go see Abuela Josie. After, I want to stop by Marvelous Millinery and clean the cabinet before my hats come back."

"Great! I'll help you," Lou Lou offered, even though she hated cleaning and doubted the cabinet was very dusty.

Pea gently lifted the new vaquera hat from the table and Lou Lou grabbed the paper bag. They went outside for the short walk, but before they left Pea's steps, Lou

Lou saw they had an unwelcome guest. Amanda Argyle was playing hopscotch on the sidewalk in front of Pea's house.

"What's *she* doing *here*?" Lou Lou asked Pea. Her ears burned.

"I have no idea. And why is she playing hopscotch by herself? That can't be very fun," Pea observed sadly.

"Pea! Don't feel bad for Amanda. She's not a nice person!" replied Lou Lou.

"I know. But still, it must be lonely," Pea said.

"I'm not lonely!" Amanda overheard and stopped hopping. "I hang out with my daddy and well . . . my daddy and . . . okay, maybe I am . . . WHATEVER! I didn't come here to talk about that. I came to tell you something important."

"What exactly would that be?" Lou Lou put her hands on her hips and gave Amanda a hard stare.

"I thought you might want to know that I love the cupcakes at Cupcake Cabana," Amanda replied. "My favorite flavor is mud pie. I go to Cupcake Cabana every Saturday to get a mud pie cupcake."

"We often go on Saturdays, too. Maybe we can go together sometime." Pea tried to be friendly.

"Wha . . . ? You'd really want to go with me?" Amanda

said. Then she shuddered as if she was shaking off a bee. "That's not the point!" she screeched.

"So what is the point?" asked Lou Lou.

"The point is that I was at Cupcake Cabana this past Saturday. You didn't see me, but I saw you."

"And?" It took Lou Lou a moment to realize the significance of this. When she did, she said, "Oh. Oh no."

"That's right. I heard everything you said. *Everything.*"

Pea's eyes went wide and Lou Lou's ears were aflame. *Chrysanthemum, chrysanthemum, chrysanthemum,* she thought, but this didn't make her any calmer.

"Daddy changed the diary to say that honeysuckle is the secret ingredient in caracoles. I guess we got it wrong when we wrote *agave,* so thanks for the correction." Amanda's tone made it clear that this wasn't a real thank-you.

"So you admit that you and your father wrote the diary! Meaning that it *is* a fake!" Lou Lou tried not to shout.

"Maybe." Amanda smirked. "But that doesn't matter anymore, does it? Now that we fixed our mistake, you have no proof. It's just your word against ours. And who is going to believe you two over my daddy, the vice-mayor of the city?"

Lou Lou didn't know what to say. Amanda was right. No one would believe Lou Lou and Pea, particularly since they'd already gotten in trouble for accidentally borrowing the diary. All Lou Lou's hopes of reclaiming the Bonanza flew off toward Verde Valley. She looked at Pea, who was at a similar loss for words.

"And since I know the secret ingredient, now *I* can definitely win the caracoles contest. Daddy decided that only Verde Valley contestants can enter." Amanda's news kept getting worse. "So you can tell your spooky friend with the weird hair to give up. Bye-bye!" As always, Amanda whipped her braids around when she began to leave. Then she turned back, whipping them in the opposite direction.

"Is that a Bonanza hat you're holding?" She pointed at the red vaquera hat. Pea clutched it protectively to her chest and shook her head. "That better be true, because the hats don't belong to you anymore. That reminds me, all of your hats look super-amazing on me!" Amanda added insult to injury.

Pea regained her powers of speech. "Yves Saint Laurent said, 'Over the years I have learned that what is important in a dress is the woman who is wearing it.' The same is true for girls and hats, Amanda. So maybe you should focus less on the Bonanza hats and more on being nicer to people."

"Good quote, Pea," Lou Lou said. She looked at Amanda. "And as Petunia Prairie said, 'Make sure to let your succulents dry out completely between waterings.'"

"Huh?" said Amanda.

"Never mind," Lou Lou replied.

Amanda whipped her braids around a third time and set off down the block.

Lou Lou's knees felt weak. She had to sit down on Pea's steps.

"This is so unfair! Our whole plan is ruined," she said. Then Lou Lou noticed Pea's tears.

"My hats," said Pea. "They're gone forever."

Lou Lou jumped up and hugged her best friend. "No!" she said. "There's got to be a way to fix this!"

"I'm not sure there is," replied Pea. "I'm afraid the bad guys might win this time, Lou Lou."

"We won't let that happen!" Lou Lou assured Pea, but she had no idea how they'd pull this off. Still, they couldn't let the bad guys win. Not on Lou Lou and Pea's watch.

CHAPTER TWENTY-TWO
Celebrar and Esperanza

Despite the horrible encounter with Amanda, Lou Lou and Pea still went to visit Abuela Josie. They decided not to ask for her help with reclaiming the Bonanza now that they had no way to expose the Argyles' lies. It was best not to risk getting into diary-related trouble again for no reason. But they wanted to give Pea's abuela her new hat and share Jeremy's caracoles.

"Oh my! ¡Es muy hermoso!" Abuela Josie said when Pea presented the vaquera hat. A tear fell from her eye and she kissed both Lou Lou and Pea on the cheek. "I have the best granddaughter in the world. And honorary granddaughter." Abuela Josie winked at Lou Lou. Lou Lou felt special being included in Pea's family, but she didn't think it was fair to take credit for her best friend's creation.

"The hat was all Pea," she said.

Pea patted Lou Lou's hand. "Thank you, but that's not true. You did an expert job with the rhinestones, Lou Lou!"

While it made Lou Lou and Pea happy to give Abuela Josie her new hat, they couldn't deny their sadness about the Bonanza. "Why the long faces?" Pea's abuela asked as they drank glasses of mango agua fresca and Abuela Josie sampled one of Jeremy's pastries. "Are you feeling down about the celebration?" Lou Lou and Pea nodded. Abuela Josie didn't even know the half of it.

"Estoy triste también." Abuela Josie sighed. "I was really looking forward to doing my stunt."

"Maybe you could perform it at my quinceañera," said Pea.

"Ah, perhaps. Pero, no me estoy haciendo más joven."

"No matter how old you are, you will always be la mejor abuela!" said Pea.

"Yeah!" agreed Lou Lou, silently apologizing to her Grandma Bombay, who was a pretty amazing grandmother, too.

Pea asked Abuela Josie to drop them off at Marvelous Millinery, even though dusting the cabinet was unnecessary now that the hats weren't coming back. When they got there, Mr. Vila was running an errand, so Pea used her key to unlock the door, told Lou Lou to wait in the showroom, and went straight to the workshop. She came back with a burgundy hat covered in magenta silk camellia blooms.

"I made this for you as a half-birthday present. I call it Pride of Pinky." Pinky was Lou Lou's blue ribbon–worthy camellia that had met an untimely end last fall.

"Oh, Pea, it's beautiful!" Lou Lou said.

"Put it on," Pea urged. "Marc Jacobs said, 'Clothes mean nothing until someone lives in them.'"

Lou Lou was too busy admiring herself in the mirror to think up a horticulture quote.

"Did you make a new one for yourself to replace . . ." Lou Lou trailed off, not wanting to mention the hat that Amanda Argyle had snatched from Pea.

"No," Pea replied. "I thought about it. But then I found the caracoles error in the diary, and I figured I would just get mine back before the Bonanza. I guess that's not true anymore." Pea took a deep breath and blew it out slowly.

"How about we go see Rosa and Helado?" Lou Lou suggested to take Pea's mind off the hat.

"That sounds nice. They always cheer me up," Pea replied.

When Lou Lou and Pea left Marvelous Millinery, they saw Rosa down the block. She was sweeping the sidewalk outside the candle shop's entrance with her bunny at her feet. Rosa looked up as Lou Lou and Pea approached and wiped her brow with the back of her hand. The fringe on the arm of her crimson blouse blew in the breeze.

"Hola, chicas!" Rosa called. "What a wonderful hat you have on, Lou Lou. ¡Me gusta mucho!"

"Gracias," Lou Lou, the hat-wearer, and Pea, the hat-maker, said simultaneously. Pea reached down to pat Helado's head.

"It was a half-birthday gift from Pea," Lou Lou added, and gently touched the hat's silk flowers.

"Have you burned your Celebrar candle?" Rosa asked.

"Not yet," replied Pea. "I'm afraid we're no closer to celebrating anything than we were when you gave it to us."

"Un momento, por favor." Rosa disappeared into the candle shop. She returned with a yellow candle that had a picture of a sun, a star, and the word *Esperanza* on the glass holder. Rosa handed it to Lou Lou.

"This one is for hope. Burn it along with the Celebrar candle and good things may come your way."

"You don't have to give us another candle," said Pea. Rosa was always giving Lou Lou and Pea candles. She said it was because they'd helped her in the past, but Rosa was actually just a nice person.

"It's nothing. Consider it a small gift for Lou Lou's half birthday," Rosa said.

"Do you really think it will help?" Lou Lou asked.

"It might," Rosa said. "And you know that tengo la intuición." She echoed a phrase that her tía Elmira had sometimes used.

"Muchas gracias, Rosa," Lou Lou said.

Since they were close to Lou Lou's house, Lou Lou and Pea went to the SS *Lucky Alley* to call Jeremy. Instead of congratulating him, they had to break the bad news about the caracoles contest. Lou Lou scurried up the rope ladder to grab the Celebrar candle from the crow's nest and they took the candles, the phone, and a snack—Lou Lou's dad's buoy chop suey—out to the backyard.

"This is terrible," said Pea. She carefully cut up her noodles while Lou Lou slurped hers down whole.

"It's not my favorite dish, but I don't think it's that bad," replied Lou Lou.

"Not the buoy chop suey, the caracoles contest," Pea said. "Jeremy was so excited about perfecting the recipe, and now he'll be heartbroken. I know just how he feels." She glanced at the Pride of Pinky hat that Lou Lou was still wearing.

"Do you want me to take it off?" Lou Lou put her hand to her head.

"Of course not," said Pea. "I miss my hats, but it makes me happy to see you wearing one."

"Okay," said Lou Lou, who'd been hoping Pea would say that. She loved her new hat and had even been wondering if she could wear it to school. El Corazón Public had a no-hats rule but surely they meant boring old baseball caps, not fabulous works of head art.

"Should we get this over with?" Pea nodded at the phone.

"Yes, but first . . ." Lou Lou slurped another noodle from her bowl and lit the Celebrar and Esperanza candles. She called Jeremy's number and held the phone out so Pea could hear, too.

"Hola, habla el mejor panadero del mundo," a voice said on the other end of the line.

"I think we have the wrong—" Lou Lou started to say.

"Hola, Jeremy," Pea said. "It's Lou Lou and Peacock. Do you always answer the phone with 'the best baker in the world speaking'?"

"Only since I perfected my caracoles recipe thanks to you two! How were they? Killer and contest-winning, I presume."

"They were perfect!" said Lou Lou. "But we have some bad news." She looked at the Celebrar and Esperanza candles and hoped for a last-minute miracle, but nothing happened.

Lou Lou and Pea told Jeremy the whole story about Amanda, the diary, and the caracoles contest. When they were finished, Jeremy was quiet. Lou Lou knew he was really disappointed because, like her, Jeremy always had something to say.

Finally he spoke. "Peacock, you won't get your hats back?" Lou Lou thought how nice it was of Jeremy to ask about Pea before thinking of himself.

"I'm afraid not." Pea's voice shook a little.

"And no one at the Bonanza will know that I mastered the caracoles recipe."

"At least *we* appreciate how great they are," replied Lou Lou. "I'm sure Rosa and Kyle will, too. You could give some to Clara the mailwoman, Mr. Vila, and even Mayor

Montoya when she gets back. There's no reason not to share them with the city even if you can't enter the contest."

Pea's eyes lit up. "You're right! That's a great idea." Lou Lou wasn't sure what part of her idea was great, but she always liked being right. "Jeremy *should* share his caracoles. He can pass out samples at the Bonanza even if he can't officially enter the contest. Lou Lou, you can wear the Pride of Pinky hat. And we'll all join in the celebration even though we're not hosting. It's still open to the whole city, right?"

"I think so," replied Lou Lou. "Andy Argyle can take the Bonanza away from El Corazón, but he hasn't said we can't attend. It's the birthday of the entire city, so we're all a part of it."

"Exactly!" said Pea. "Maybe we need to change the way we look at this. The Bonanza is not about El Corazón versus Verde Valley, it's about celebrating our entire city."

"That's a lovely thought, Peacock Pearl!" Jeremy said. "And it sounds reasonable to me. Especially if I get to bring my killer caracoles! Let's go show our city pride!"

"I'm sure we can get other people to come, too! What do you think, Lou Lou?" asked Pea.

Lou Lou admired Pea's generous spirit, and she knew what Pea said made sense. She saw no way to stop the Argyles, so they should make the best of the Bonanza situation. Lou Lou was still angry that the vice-mayor was being so unfair, and this felt like letting the Argyles win. But wouldn't Amanda and her father be winning even bigger if she and Pea moped around and didn't go to their city's birthday celebration? Lou Lou looked at the Celebrar and Esperanza candles. This wasn't the miracle she'd hoped for, but maybe it was good enough.

"Okay," Lou Lou said. "I'm in!"

CHAPTER TWENTY-THREE
Fellow Feline Fancier

The Bonanza was the following weekend, so Lou Lou and Pea had little time to rally El Corazón friends and neighbors to put aside their hurt feelings and instead show their city pride. It was easy to tell Rosa, Juan, their schoolmates, and other people they saw regularly, but they wanted to reach a bigger crowd. Luckily, Sarah agreed to add a message to the Bonanza mural that said: ¡TODAVÍA SOMOS PARTE DE LA CIUDAD! WE ARE STILL PART OF THE CITY! And in smaller letters: *Celebren con Verde Valley el 20 Mayo! Celebrate with Verde Valley on May 20th!*

Lou Lou and Pea also pooled their saved allowances to put an announcement in the neighborhood newspaper, *La Voz de El Corazón*. Between the money in Lou Lou's whale-shaped silver bank and Pea's savings from her blue box under her bed, they scraped up twenty-nine dollars and fifty-one cents. Lou Lou thought this was an impressive sum until they arrived at *La Voz*'s office after school on Monday.

"Sorry, announcements start at thirty-five dollars," the woman at the front desk said without looking up from her magazine.

"But it's for something important!" Pea replied.

"About the Bonanza!" Lou Lou added.

"Mmhmm, there's nothing I can do for you," said the woman. "Besides, haven't you heard? The Bonanza belongs to Verde Valley now."

Pea peeked over the desk at the woman's magazine. "I see you are reading *Cat Connoisseur*, Ms."—Lou Lou nodded at the woman's nameplate—"Adelaide Stout. Are you a feline fancier?"

"I am." Adelaide Stout finally looked up. "I have three Persians, two Maine coons, and one British shorthair."

"What a coincidence. I have both a Persian and a British shorthair," Pea said.

"¿En serio?" Ms. Stout smiled. "It's so nice to meet a fellow fancier. What did you say you wanted again?" Pea explained one more time.

"Let's see about getting that announcement printed!" Ms. Stout said.

·>> • <<·

First thing the next morning, Lou Lou grabbed the copy of *La Voz* from the doorstep of the SS *Lucky Alley*. Sure enough, on page three, there was their announcement:

COME ONE, COME ALL
COME BIG, COME SMALL
TO MARK OUR CITY'S SPECIAL DAY
ON THE TWENTIETH OF MAY
OUR HOSTING DUTIES MET THEIR END
BUT THAT DOESN'T MEAN WE CAN'T ATTEND
SO EL CORAZÓN, DON'T DILLYDALLY
GET YOURSELVES TO VERDE VALLEY
(FOR THE BICENTENNIAL BONANZA!)
SEE YOU THERE!
YOUR FRIENDS,
LOU LOU BOMBAY AND PEACOCK PEARL

Lou Lou smiled. They'd borrowed a bit from Ella Divine's song, but she and Pea had made up the rest. And it was a pretty good announcement, if Lou Lou did say so herself. They'd wanted to add something about the gazebo, but the only word they could find to rhyme was *placebo*. Neither of them knew what that meant, so they decided against it.

"I'm proud of you, honey." Lou Lou hadn't realized her mom was reading over her shoulder until she spoke. "It's great you are encouraging everyone to go to the Bonanza this weekend, particularly after that unfortunate business with the diary."

"Thanks, Mom." Lou Lou still hoped deep down that they could find a way to foil the Argyles' scheme, but it felt good to know that they would be celebrating their city's two hundredth birthday no matter what.

It seemed that Lou Lou and Pea's announcement caught the attention of more than just Lou Lou's mom. That week, the neighborhood was abuzz with talk of the Bonanza.

"We're planning to go," Lou Lou overheard one woman say at La Frutería when Lou Lou was buying her after-school papaya. "Even though I'm still upset that we won't have the gazebo for our knitting circle meetings, it's our city, too, after all." Pea reported that she'd overheard people on the bus and on the street talking excitedly about the celebration, too.

On Friday, Lou Lou ran into Jeremy in the hall after Math class.

"Hi! What are you doing on the fifth-grade floor?" she asked, narrowly avoiding bumping into him but dropping her math book.

"Looking for you!" Jeremy picked up her book, and a bright red spike of his hair flopped into his face.

"You're still coming on Saturday, right?"

"Um, yeah!" Jeremy said as if Lou Lou was silly to even ask. "And I'll be wearing this!" Jeremy opened his leather jacket to reveal a black T-shirt with silver letters that read *Jeremy's Killer Caracoles* above a picture of the pastry.

"I like it!" said Lou Lou.

"I'm glad to hear that," Jeremy replied. "Because I made one for both you and Peacock." He opened his messenger bag and pulled out two shirts. One was bright red and the

other was light blue, but otherwise they matched Jeremy's shirt.

"Wow, thanks!" Lou Lou replied, thinking the shirt would look funny with the Pride of Pinky hat she also planned to wear. But Lou Lou didn't mind looking a little funny.

"Gotta go. I've got Music class next, and my fallback profession is rock star if this baker thing doesn't work out! See you Saturday, Lou Lou Bombay!" Jeremy turned and loped off down the hall. Lou Lou put the blue T-shirt into her satchel and slipped the red one over her flowered sweater. There was no reason to wait until the weekend to show her support for Jeremy's killer caracoles!

CHAPTER TWENTY-FOUR
Bonanza-Bound

As the time until the Bonanza got shorter and shorter, Lou Lou's excitement grew bigger and bigger. She looked forward to eating Jeremy's killer caracoles and watching the festivities, even though her friends and neighbors were no longer the performers and hosts. Her anger at the Argyles had gone from a boil to a low simmer. It was still there beneath the surface, but at least it wasn't stopping her from happily anticipating the weekend's events. Lou Lou knew her frustration would return when she saw Pea's stolen hats and the gazebo that should have been in Limonero Park. But for now, she was excited to celebrate her city.

Pea slept over at the SS *Lucky Alley* on Friday night. After a yummy dinner that ended with porthole pecan pie, Lou Lou and Pea went to bed so they'd be well rested for the special day.

·>> • <<·

The girls awoke bright-eyed the next morning and started getting ready. "I brought a few outfits so you can help me decide what to wear." Pea pointed to her overstuffed duffel. She always came well prepared.

"I almost forgot!" Lou Lou said. She took the blue T-shirt Jeremy had made out of her satchel and grabbed her red shirt as well. Pea laughed when she held them up.

"He's really getting into the killer caracoles spirit!" she said. "But he doesn't actually expect us to wear these, right?"

Lou Lou raised her eyebrows. "Um . . ." she said.

"Oh no! He does! But it has no style or shape to it whatsoever!"

"I'll wear mine," Lou Lou said. "But I'm sure it's okay if you don't wear yours. Jeremy will understand that you can't compromise your fashion sense."

"No," said Pea. "I don't want him to be offended. As

Yves Saint Laurent said, 'We must never confuse elegance with snobbery.'"

"Well, Lloyd Lavender said, 'Just because you love petunias doesn't mean you have to wear them to a party.'"

Pea was too busy elaborately folding the shirt to applaud Lou Lou's appropriate horticulture quote. When she was done, Pea tied it around her neck, creating an elegant kerchief.

Lou Lou clapped her hands. "Perfect!" she said. She placed Pride of Pinky on her head, and Pea smiled.

"It's too bad we can't admire your honeysuckle today, Lou Lou."

"I know," Lou Lou replied. "But I'm bringing this to remind myself how beautiful the plants look in Limonero Park." She carefully put a honeysuckle cutting into her satchel.

Lou Lou changed into jeans and helped Pea select pants and a shirt dotted with blue flowers. Afterward, they went down-ladder for a pre-Bonanza breakfast of banana pancakes. It was a Bombay Saturday morning, after all.

When they finished eating, Lou Lou quickly checked on her sprouting peonies and daffodils. Then she and Pea were ready to go.

"Mom! Dad! Are you coming?" Lou Lou called to her parents. "It's time to be Bonanza-bound!"

"Aye, aye, First Mate Lou Lou and Quartermaster Peacock," Lou Lou's dad replied.

Pea looked at Lou Lou. "What's a—"

"Ask him later," Lou Lou interrupted. "We don't have time for an explanation of nautical terms. We have to be at the park by five bells." Pea laughed.

Minutes later, the Bombays and Pea were in the car. It was only a ten-minute drive to La Fuente Park, a large square of grass in the center of Verde Valley that was only slightly smaller than Limonero Park. La Fuente Park didn't have Limonero Park's beautiful lemon trees, but it was still lovely with its laurel trees filled with birds and a rose garden that Lou Lou had always admired. When they arrived, there were already many people there.

"Looks like a good turnout from El Corazón!" said Lou Lou's mom. It was true that many of their friends and neighbors had come for the morning's Bonanza festivities. Danielle and her snooty-girl posse were there, as were Sarah, Rosa, and Mr. Vila. Pea waved at Adelaide Stout, the feline fancier.

Lou Lou and Pea stopped to say hello to Thomas from

Sparkle 'N Clean, and he complimented Pea on her unusual kerchief.

Pea replied, "As Coco Chanel said, 'In order to be irreplaceable, one must always be different.'"

Lou Lou was eager to join the crowd assembling for the caracoles contest, and she hopped impatiently from foot to foot as her parents chatted with Thomas.

"I've been meaning to stop by the boutique to talk to you about a sailor suit I'd like to special order," Lou Lou's dad said. Her mom noticed Lou Lou's let's-go-now dance.

"You and Pea run on ahead, honey," said Jane. "We'll catch up." Lou Lou kissed her mom on the cheek.

Lou Lou and Pea headed toward a small stage that was surrounded by a semicircle of chairs. On the stage was a tall, shiny trophy topped with a silver caracol. A banner that said CARACOLES CONTEST! ONLY VERDE VALLEY BAKERS MAY ENTER! hung over the stage. The welcome banners that Lou Lou's very own art class had made were stretched between two trees. Lou Lou's ears reddened. But she said her *chrysanthemum*s and took deep breaths. She was absolutely determined to make the best of the Bonanza and their city's special day!

CHAPTER TWENTY-FIVE
Caracoles Contest

Lou Lou and Pea saw Kyle on their way to the Bonanza stage. He was wearing his Comet Cop cape and had brought his dog, Mars Rover. In a tribute to Kyle's long-lost space goats, Mars Rover wore a tinfoil helmet. He didn't look happy, but at least he wasn't eating it as an early lunch.

"Hi, guys. I mean, greetings, Earthlings." Kyle waved his arms frantically as if Lou Lou and Pea might miss him. With the cape, the dog, the helmet, and the fact that Kyle was standing right in front of Lou Lou and Pea, this was nearly impossible.

"Hey, Kyle," Lou Lou said. She noticed a dollop of cream in the corner of Kyle's mouth.

Pea didn't miss it either. "Have you been eating caracoles?"

"Affirmative! The ones on your shirt." Kyle pointed at Lou Lou.

"What?" Lou Lou remembered she was wearing Jeremy's *Killer Caracoles* T-shirt. "Where is Jeremy?"

Kyle pointed and Lou Lou saw Jeremy, wearing his own black T-shirt and holding a platter heaped with his killer caracoles. From the crowd surrounding him, Lou Lou could tell that the platter would quickly be empty. People were gobbling up his pastries and coming back for seconds. Jeremy wore an ear-to-ear goofy grin.

"We should get one before he runs out," Pea said. "But first, where's the gazebo? Isn't it supposed to be revealed at the festivities?"

"Good question. I thought so, too. Maybe it'll be here later? Or maybe—" Before Lou Lou could finish her sentence, she noticed a commotion around Jeremy.

"I will not stand for your unauthorized distribution of caracoles, young man!" a voice boomed.

"Uh-oh," Lou Lou said. "It sounds like Andy Argyle discovered Jeremy's killer caracoles." Sure enough, through a break in the crowd, Lou Lou saw the vice-mayor talking to Jeremy. Andy Argyle wore a flashy purple-and-gold-argyle-print suit and his usual shiny shoes. He twirled the end of his goatee angrily.

"Rather garish." Pea looked disapprovingly at the vice-mayor's attire.

Jeremy said something that Lou Lou couldn't hear. But she guessed from his jutted-out chin and narrowed eyes that Jeremy wasn't being agreeable. With one quick sweep of his arm, Andy Argyle knocked Jeremy's remaining caracoles off his tray. There was a gasp from the crowd, and Lou Lou's ears were instantly hot.

"Hey!" she yelled, marching over to stand beside Jeremy. "What do you think you're doing?"

"You again!" shouted the vice-mayor. "I'm not surprised that *you're* here messing up *my* day! If you must know, I am enforcing the rules of the caracoles contest."

He pointed to the banner above the stage. "Only Verde Valley bakers may enter!"

"But Jeremy wasn't entering the contest," said Pea, who had joined Lou Lou. "He was simply sharing his killer caracoles with the crowd. So he's not actually breaking the rules."

"Well—no—I—I don't have to explain myself to you!" Andy Argyle sputtered. "I've half a mind to kick you both out of La Fuente Park right this moment."

"You can't just—" Lou Lou began.

"It's okay, Lou Lou," Jeremy said. "Vice-Mayor, I'm sorry about the caracoles." From his crossed fingers behind his back, Lou Lou could tell he wasn't truly sorry. "I just thought I'd give everyone a pre-contest snack. To get them excited about the main event, ya know? Surely you don't want to kick us out now that Mayor Montoya has arrived."

"Mayor Montoya!" Lou Lou said.

"She's back?" Pea asked.

"What? Where?!" Andy Argyle exclaimed.

Jeremy pointed at the mayor, who was smiling and waving to the crowd as she made her way toward the stage. Secretly stealing the Bonanza from El Corazón was one thing, but it wouldn't look good if Mayor

Montoya saw Andy Argyle banning people from the city-wide celebration.

"Just stay out of my sight and don't cause any more trouble!" Andy Argyle spun on his shiny heel and stomped off.

"I hope the mayor's return means Putt Putt the puli is all better," said Pea.

"Mayor Montoya can help us get the Bonanza back!" Lou Lou still wasn't ready to give up. "Then Jeremy can enter the caracoles contest."

"¡Ya quisiera!" Jeremy said. "I know my caracoles would beat Amanda's hands down even though she also knows the secret ingredient. But I think it's too late for me. The contest is about to begin!"

"And we don't have any proof now that the diary is a fake, remember?" Pea pointed out. "So there's no reason the mayor would help us reclaim the Bonanza."

Lou Lou realized that Jeremy and Pea were right. She just couldn't stop hoping that things would work out. She and Pea helped Jeremy pick up the scattered caracoles from the ground.

"They're only a little dirty; we could probably still eat them," said Lou Lou. Pea crinkled her nose.

Jeremy laughed. "No need. I've got a whole backup stash." He patted his messenger bag. "I thought demand would be high, so I made extra. I'll give you one when I'm certain Patrick Plaid or Harold Houndstooth or whatever that guy's name is isn't watching." Andy Argyle was out of earshot but, as if on cue, he flashed Jeremy, Lou Lou, and Pea a look of warning.

"Attention!" Mayor Montoya stood at a microphone at the front of the stage. "We'll begin in just a moment." Lou Lou and Pea found seats near Sarah and Rosa. Lou Lou spotted a flash of red and nudged Pea.

"Look, there's Abuela Josie! She's wearing her new hat!"

"It looks magnificent!" Lou Lou and Pea waved at Pea's abuela. Abuela Josie pointed at her hat and blew them a kiss.

The crowd quieted and Mayor Montoya said, "Greetings, everyone! I am very pleased that I could return to my city in time for this historic occasion! You will be happy to know that Putt Putt the puli made a full recovery."

Pea smiled. "That's something to be grateful for today," she said.

"I was surprised to find out that we would be celebrating in Verde Valley and not El Corazón," continued the mayor. "But Vice-Mayor Argyle explained about the diary and the founders' decree, and I understand that his hands were tied when it came to the Bonanza's location."

"Not exactly," grumbled Lou Lou.

"Now, without further ado," said Mayor Montoya. "Bienvenidos to the opening event of our city's Bicentennial Bonanza, the caracoles contest!"

Andy Argyle took over the microphone. "Yes, I suppose we are very fortunate that Mayor Montoya has returned in time to co-judge the caracoles contest." He sounded anything but sincere.

"Gracias, Vice-Mayor." Mayor Montoya gave a little bow. The crowd clapped excitedly.

"As Bicentennial Bonanza Boss—" Andy Argyle began. Mayor Montoya cleared her throat, and the vice-mayor looked at her out of the corner of his eye. "I mean as Bicentennial Bonanza Vice-Boss, I will, of course, be the other judge." Andy Argyle was clearly annoyed about being second-in-command again.

"That's not fair. He shouldn't be a judge," Lou Lou whispered. She hadn't even considered who would be judging the caracoles contest, although it wasn't surprising that Andy Argyle had appointed himself.

"It means Amanda will have a huge advantage even if her caracoles aren't the best," Pea whispered back. "At least the mayor won't be biased."

"As you all know, the caracoles champion will have the honor of serving our famous local pastry at the Bonanza," the vice-mayor said. "¡Qi comenchen la concursa di caracoles!"

Lou Lou raised her eyebrows at Pea.

"I think he means *¡Que comience el concurso de caracoles!* Let the caracoles contest begin!" Pea said. "But the only word he got right was *caracoles*."

Lou Lou giggled. At the very least, she could relish

the fact that she spoke Spanish better than the vice-mayor.

"I guess we'll see whether Amanda can pull off making good caracoles," Lou Lou said.

"Yes, this should be interesting," Pea replied.

As it turned out, Pea was right. But Lou Lou and Pea were soon to discover that they didn't even know the half of it!

CHAPTER TWENTY-SIX
You Can't Eat That!

"Our first caracoles contestant is Monsieur Bonsoir, owner of Verde Valley Bistro," Andy Argyle announced.

A man stood up in the front row. He wore a chef's hat and a white jacket and held a large brown paper bag full of *caracoles*. He handed one to each of the judges and they both took a bite while the crowd watched eagerly for a reaction. Mayor Montoya nodded and jotted something down on a notepad. Andy Argyle looked out into the audience and made certain everyone saw his frown. After Monsieur Bonsoir returned to his seat, the vice-mayor spoke into the microphone again.

"Next up is Gertrude Alvarado," he said. No one moved, so Andy Argyle peered out into the audience. "Gertrude, are you here? GERTRUDE!" he yelled. Finally, a little old lady stood up.

"I'm here," she called nervously. "But I just realized that I left my tin of caracoles at home. Perhaps I can go—"

"Disqualified!" The vice-mayor stamped his shiny-shoed foot and Gertrude's face crumpled.

"Pobrecita. I wish we could give her a hug," Pea whispered.

"I don't think disqualification is necessary, Vice-Mayor Argyle." Mayor Montoya flashed him a disapproving look.

"Right." Andy Argyle cleared his throat and looked back at Gertrude. "Because I am incredibly kind, I will allow you to fetch your caracoles and return."

Andy Argyle called more contestants and the contest continued. Lou Lou glanced at Jeremy to see if he seemed angry about being excluded. He was munching heartily on one of his own killer caracoles.

"Numbing my pain with sugar," he said when he caught Lou Lou's eye. He flashed a goofy grin and she smiled back.

"Now for the moment we've all been waiting for!" Andy Argyle said, and Lou Lou turned her attention back to the stage. "The next contestant is my darling daughter, Amanda Argyle!"

"Ugh," Lou Lou said to Pea.

Amanda simpered, then practically pranced up to the stage to join her father. She wore a green-and-pink-argyle-print jumper, and her hair was in her usual braids. Even though the Bonanza hats would be given out to the crowd later that day, Amanda was already wearing Pea's blue hat. Even Lou Lou could tell that the lovely hat clashed horribly with Amanda's outfit. Lou Lou's ears grew hotter by the second. She noticed Pea biting her bottom lip.

"I expected her to be wearing it, but I didn't realize it would make me so sad and angry." Pea shook her head. "I'm not going to let it ruin this day," she said with renewed determination.

Amanda stood next to her father holding a tray covered with a red-and-white-argyle-print cloth. She had the fake diary tucked under her arm.

"I have a feeling these caracoles are going to be extra special," Andy Argyle said to the crowd.

Amanda pulled the cloth dramatically off the tray

to reveal the pastries underneath like she was doing a magic trick. She handed the tray and cloth to her father so she could get closer to the microphone.

"They're extra special because we know the secret ingredient!" she boasted. "It's in Giles's diary!" She waved the little book in the air.

"Darling, perhaps we should wait until—" Andy Argyle started to say. But Amanda was unstoppable. She had to brag about what she knew right then and there.

"The secret ingredient is honeysuckle berries!" she cried, and handed a caracol to Mayor Montoya. Lou Lou's anger was starting to get the better of her. *How dare Amanda brag about the recipe!* Lou Lou thought. *How dare Amanda wear Pea's hat!*

"Lou Lou," Pea's voice cut into Lou Lou's thoughts.

How dare the Argyles lie about Giles's diary!

"Lou Lou!"

How dare they take the Bicentennial from El Corazón!

Lou Lou took a deep breath and said her *chrysanthemums*. "Yes?" she finally answered.

"Did you hear Amanda?"

"Of course, and I can't believe the nerve of—"

"No, no," Pea interrupted. "She said the secret

ingredient is honeysuckle *berries*, not honeysuckle *nectar*. Didn't you tell us that you can eat honeysuckle nectar, but honeysuckle berries are—"

"POISONOUS!" Lou Lou shouted.

The crowd turned in their seats to look at her.

"What did I tell you about causing trouble, little girl?" Andy Argyle boomed at Lou Lou. But Lou Lou wasn't paying attention to him. She was staring white-faced at Mayor Montoya, who clearly hadn't heard Lou Lou and was lifting her caracol to her lips.

"YOU CAN'T EAT THAT!" Pea stood up and shouted even louder than Lou Lou. Pea never raised her voice except for something very important. Mayor Montoya's hand froze in midair.

"Don't listen to her! Take a bite!" Amanda shrieked. Mayor Montoya seemed unsure of what to do, and she moved the pastry toward her mouth again. Lou Lou regained her composure.

"NO!" she yelled. "HONEYSUCKLE BERRIES ARE POISONOUS!"

The mayor raised her eyebrows. Her mouth formed an O and her arm went rigid. Mayor Montoya dropped the caracol onto the stage and came to stand next to the Argyles at the microphone.

"Is this true?" Mayor Montoya asked.

"Yes!" Lou Lou heard Juan call from the far side of the crowd.

"I don't understand," Mayor Montoya said. "Why would Giles's diary say the secret ingredient is honeysuckle berries if they're poisonous?"

Both the vice-mayor and his daughter seemed to be at a complete loss for words. "I . . . uh . . . um," Andy Argyle replied in a not-so-booming voice.

"Because the diary is a fake!" Pea cried.

"The Argyles forged the whole thing!" Jeremy shouted.

Principal Garcia stood up and looked at the vice-mayor, aghast. "So the girls were right about the diary the whole time?" he asked.

Pea squeezed Lou Lou's arm hopefully.

"'Fake'? 'Forged'? 'Right about the diary'?" Mayor Montoya asked. "What's going on here?"

Principal Garcia quickly explained the situation.

"No, of course they weren't right." Andy Argyle glared at Lou Lou and Pea, then smiled unconvincingly at

Principal Garcia and the mayor. "I'm sure Giles just made an error when he wrote down the recipe."

"That's not true!" Lou Lou yelled. "We know the real secret ingredient, and we've got a caracoles contestant to prove it!" Lou Lou didn't have to signal Jeremy. He was already heading for the stage. He pulled his backup killer caracoles out of his messenger bag and handed a pastry to Mayor Montoya.

"But his are made with honeysuckle, too, so you can't eat them either!" Amanda said. She looked at Jeremy. "Ha! Gotcha!"

"Honeysuckle *nectar*, not honeysuckle *berries*," Jeremy said.

"The nectar is not poisonous," Lou Lou called.

"¡Es verdad!" Juan confirmed. "In fact, it's great in tea."

"That's a wonderful idea," Pea said to Lou Lou. "We should try honeysuckle nectar in our PSPP tea!"

Mayor Montoya took a big bite of Jeremy's caracol, then gobbled the whole thing down. "We have a winner!" she declared. "Muy muy delicioso and just like our dearly departed Señora Basa used to make at her panadería! How did you know to use the nectar?"

"It's all thanks to Peacock Pearl, proud resident of El

Corazón and direct descendant of Diego Soto," Jeremy replied. "She gave me the *real* recipe!"

The crowd looked at Pea and she smiled.

"His caracoles might be good, but let's not get carried away! I don't see how a silly mistake and a lucky guess at the secret ingredient changes anything or proves that the diary is a fake!" Andy Argyle said angrily.

"Perhaps I could have a look at that?" Mayor Montoya took the diary from Amanda and flipped through the pages. "Hmm, I've seen Giles's handwriting on the city charter and this is *not* it."

Andy Argyle nervously twirled the end of his goatee. "Mayor Montoya, if I could just—"

"This certainly doesn't look good, Mr. Vice-Mayor," Mayor Montoya interrupted. "A fake diary, plus, Amanda almost poisoned me. That's no way to kick off the Bonanza." The mayor frowned. "Do *you* have any explanation for this?"

Before Andy Argyle could reply, a large delivery truck pulled up alongside the park and honked loudly. Lou Lou, Pea, and the rest of the crowd turned to look. On the side of the truck, in big orange letters, was written SAMMY'S GAZEBO DELIVERY. A man, presumably Sammy, leaned out of the driver's-side window.

"Hey there, Vice-Mayor Argyle!" Sammy yelled. "I tried to deliver the gazebo to your backyard like you asked, but your gate was locked. I can try again tomorrow or you can give me a key."

"Did he just say he tried to deliver the gazebo to *your backyard*?" Mayor Montoya asked in disbelief. Lou Lou's ears turned a cherry color.

"Yes . . . well . . . um . . . you see . . ." Andy Argyle said.

Lou Lou thought about all the gazebo paraphernalia in the vice-mayor's office. Clearly, he wanted the gazebo for himself! Then she suddenly remembered what they'd overheard at the Heliotrope. "Pea, the night of the Preview, Andy Argyle said something about the gazebo and a backyard!"

Pea nodded. "I know. We didn't think much of it at the time but—"

Mayor Montoya's voice cut off Pea. "Why would the gazebo be going in your backyard?"

"Yeah, por qué?" someone in the crowd yelled.

"The official city rules for the Bonanza say that Verde Valley can chose the location for the gazebo. We chose my—"

"¡No es verdad! Verde Valley didn't choose your

backyard. *You* did," cried another audience member. "The gazebo is for the whole community to enjoy, not for just you! It should go in the park!"

"No! No! NO!" screamed Amanda. "The gazebo is for us because Daddy is a gazebo enthusiast! That's why we moved the Bonanza to Verde Valley in the first place—so Daddy could have the gazebo. And so I could wear pretty hats so that people would like me! And to show you that stupid El Corazón isn't as lovely as you think it is, even though you're all so . . . nice!"

"Amanda, darling, please stop talking!" said Andy

Argyle. But it was too late. The secret was out that the Argyles had planned to keep the beautiful gazebo all to themselves.

"Well, I never!" Mayor Montoya shouted. "This is outrageous, Vice-Mayor Argyle. I'm disappointed in you. I thought you were an honorable person. A bit odd and flashy, yes, but not unjust and devious. And you assured me that you could be a good leader, not just someone who shows up to ribbon cuttings and kisses babies at parades."

"Joke's on you! He's devious AND he doesn't even like babies!" shouted Amanda. Mayor Montoya ignored her.

"As of right now, you are hereby relieved of all duties as vice-mayor, Mr. Argyle," said Mayor Montoya. "Do you have anything to say for yourself?" It seemed that Andy Argyle had nothing to say because he'd taken Amanda by the elbow and was heading for his car.

It took a moment for everything to sink in, but then Lou Lou said, "We did it!"

"We proved that the diary is a fake!"

"Good riddance to the Argyles! Enemies of the universe."

Lou Lou, Pea, and Kyle were all talking at once. Lou Lou could hardly believe it. Just when she thought all hope of exposing the Argyles was lost, everything had turned around. Lou Lou felt like cheering, but there was one more step to justice and victory.

"Mayor Montoya, does this mean the Bonanza belongs to El Corazón again?" Lou Lou asked.

"Without the diary, there's nothing linking the celebration solely to Verde Valley, so the answer is yes," the mayor answered.

"Great! So we can move the festivities back to—"

"Lou Lou," Pea interrupted for the second time that morning. She eyed the crowd. "Maybe we should come up with a different plan."

Lou Lou looked around at the faces of the audience. Her El Corazón friends and neighbors were grinning. Juan waved, and Lou Lou's dad gave her a sea captain's salute. Danielle and her snooty-girl posse were already practicing their dance moves. But the people from Verde Valley looked crestfallen. Lou Lou remembered how it had felt to lose the Bonanza to Verde Valley. She imagined that the Verde Valley residents probably felt similarly now that El Corazón was set to reclaim the celebration at the very last minute.

Pea raised her hand. "I have an idea, Mayor Montoya. Since both neighborhoods have prepared for the Bonanza, what if El Corazón and Verde Valley share it?" A murmur went through the audience.

As usual, Lou Lou was impressed by Pea's selflessness.

"We could have the Bonanza here in La Fuente Park, and El Corazón can pitch in for the celebration!" Lou Lou said. She thought of her honeysuckle in Limonero Park. Lou Lou wanted everyone to see her beautiful plants, and unsurprisingly Amanda hadn't managed to grow any Verde Valley honeysuckle. But Juan could just bring over the extra potted honeysuckle from Green Thumb. Pea squeezed Lou Lou's hand, and she felt a rush of pride at doing the right thing.

"¡Creo que es una solución genial!" Rosa said as she stood up.

"Me too!" Sarah was on her feet. It wasn't long before the whole crowd was standing and shouting.

"Let's do it!"

"¡Una idea maravillosa!"

"We can both host the Bonanza!"

"So what do you think, Mayor Montoya?" Thomas asked.

"I think that's un plan fantástico," replied the Mayor. "We will hold the Bonanza here in Verde Valley, and both neighborhoods will co-host the festivities."

Pea clapped and Lou Lou let out a cheer. The rest of the audience followed suit. When the commotion died down, Jeremy said, "Well, now that that's settled, let's get back to my killer caracoles. You mentioned something about a winner."

"That's right," said Mayor Montoya. "It's you!" She handed Jeremy the shiny trophy. He grinned and raised it high above his head. Applause erupted in the crowd again, and Lou Lou and Pea were the loudest of all.

CHAPTER TWENTY-SEVEN
Blue Beauty

Lou Lou and Pea felt exhilarated after the caracoles contest. But they didn't have time for a happy dance or a celebratory cupcake because there were so many things to do. The contest ended at eleven-thirty, and the Bonanza celebration started that afternoon at four. That meant there were only a few hours for everyone to work together to make sure this was the best Bicentennial Bonanza celebration a city had ever seen!

La Fuente Park began to fill with even more people setting up for the festivities. Sarah hung Bonanza papel picado and balloons. Ella Divine practiced a duet with

Ruby Sol, Verde Valley's best-loved singer. Kyle was finally reunited with his beloved space goats, and he and Tommy worked together to be sure Jupiter didn't eat his helmet.

The first thing Lou Lou and Pea did was look around for Mr. Vila to ask him about the return of the hats. But it appeared he'd left the park right after the caracoles contest.

"If the Argyles have your hats, how will we get them back?" Lou Lou asked. "I doubt they'll show their faces at the Bonanza later." Lou Lou and Pea had always assumed the hats would be returned with the Bonanza, but since Andy Argyle said he was personally keeping them until the celebration, they hadn't really thought this through.

"I don't know," said Pea. "Mr. Vila is probably working on that now." She smiled, but Lou Lou could tell she was concerned.

"I'm sure you're right." Lou Lou patted Pea's arm and hoped this was true. After their hard work to reclaim the Bonanza, it would be terrible if Pea didn't get her hats back.

Lou Lou's parents drove Lou Lou and Pea back to El Corazón so they could get things ready for the celebration. The first stop was Green Thumb, where Lou Lou and Juan chose the finest potted honeysuckle to bring to La Fuente Park. Afterward, Lou Lou and Pea headed to Marvelous Millinery to look for Mr. Vila. As they were walking to the hat shop from the greenhouse, a tiny car pulled up beside them. The car's unusual plum color and old-fashioned style made it recognizable anywhere.

"Mr. Vila!" Lou Lou and Pea exclaimed when the milliner rolled down the window and poked his head out.

"Greetings, Peacock. Hello there, Lou Lou. Lovely day day for a Bicentennial Bonanza, don't you think? And aren't we lucky that El Corazón gets to co-host?"

"Absolutely," said Pea. "Mr. Vila, I wanted to ask—"

"The hats, Mr. Vila! Where are the hats?" Lou Lou blurted out.

"Never fear, Lou Lou. I have just come from La Fuente Park where I have left all the hats hats so that they are ready for the Bonanza."

Pea's eyes lit up. "¡Que buenas noticias! I was so worried we wouldn't get them back from the Argyles!" she said.

"That wouldn't be right, now, would it?" said Mr. Vila. "Vice-Mayor Argyle was keeping the hats in a closet at

City Hall. Even Mayor Montoya didn't have a key key but hatpins make excellent lock picks." Mr. Vila winked.

"Wow!" Lou Lou was impressed with the hatter's resourcefulness.

"I thought you might like to have this one right right away." Mr. Vila lifted something from the passenger seat and passed it to Pea through the window. It was Abuela Josie's lucky hat.

"Mr. Vila, you're a hero!" Pea exclaimed.

"One one thing, though," said Mr. Vila. "I couldn't get back the hat you made for yourself, Peacock, as that dreadful girl is still wearing it. Which is why you need to come with me to the hat shop. Quick quick. We don't have much time before the Bonanza."

Lou Lou and Pea hopped into the backseat of Mr. Vila's funny little car to drive the few blocks to Marvelous Millinery. On the way, Pea called Abuela Josie, who was thrilled to hear that her lucky hat had been returned. She was heading to the stables because she'd be performing her one-foot-drag, around-the-world combo after all.

Inside the hat shop, Mr. Vila said, "Wait wait right here. I'll be back in a jiffy." He disappeared into the workshop and reemerged a moment later holding a hatbox. On it was a gift tag that read *For Peacock Pearl, the Best Best Milliner's Apprentice That Ever There Was*. Pea took the top off the box and lifted out a beautiful hat. It had a huge light blue straw brim and a royal blue feathered ribbon curlicue on the side. The top of the hat was embroidered with navy polka dots. It was elegant and eye-catching—perfect for Pea!

"Gorgeous!" Lou Lou gasped.

Pea was speechless. Finally she said, "Oh Mr. Vila, it's truly extraordinario! Muchas gracias a million times over!" Pea put on the hat and looked in the mirror. "Christian Dior said, 'Pale blue is one of the prettiest colors, and if you have blue eyes no color is more becoming.'"

"He was right!" Lou Lou replied. "Your hat needs a name, Pea. Mine's Pride of Pinky, so what should yours be?"

Pea closed her eyes and thought for a second. "I'll call it Blue Beauty," she said.

"Perfect!" replied Lou Lou. "Bicentennial Bonanza, here come Lou Lou and Pea!"

CHAPTER TWENTY-EIGHT
¡Gracias por el Mirador!

By four o'clock that afternoon, a giant crowd had filled La Fuente Park for the main Bonanza events: the performances and citywide celebration. Not only were there participants and spectators from both El Corazón and Verde Valley, but also from the other neighborhoods in the city. The park looked amazing. Sarah's decorations were complemented by Jane Bombay's origami birthday cakes. There were colorful paintings showing streets, festivals, and landmarks, as well as the photographs from the City Archives and the painting of Diego and his horse, which Pea had brought for the occasion. Rosa's

Celebrar candles were everywhere, waiting to be lit once the sun set. Lou Lou and Pea helped Juan place the honeysuckle plants around the edges of the park. Mayor Montoya joined them as Lou Lou was pruning one of the bushes.

"¡Su madreselva es muy bonita!" Mayor Montoya said.

Lou Lou recognized the words *honeysuckle* and *pretty* and grinned. "¡Gracias!" she replied.

"I can't thank you both enough for warning me about the honeysuckle berries and figuring out the diary was a fake," Mayor Montoya said to Lou Lou and Pea. "I promise to find a way to honor you for helping our city root out injustice. Les debo mucho."

Lou Lou's ears went pink with excitement, and when the mayor was gone, she elbowed Pea. "Did you hear that? She'll find a way to honor us!" The day just kept getting better.

When they'd finished with the honeysuckle, Lou Lou, Pea, and Mr. Vila gave out hats to the Bonanza participants. Lou Lou and Pea knew the hats were beautiful, but they were an even bigger hit with the crowd than they'd imagined.

"Ooh!" said a group of people when Pea handed out the hats representing the different city neighborhoods.

"Ah!" Another group marveled at the exact replica of Giles's jaunty cap. There weren't enough hats to go around, but everyone happily took turns wearing one of Mr. Vila and Pea's gorgeous creations.

The Bonanza performances kicked off with a song from Ella Divine and Ruby Sol. Lou Lou and Pea sat on the grass on Pea's checkered blanket to watch. Next up was Abuela Josie performing her famous stunt. Pea's abuela came into the park with her horse at a full gallop, wearing her lucky vaquera hat. Pea knit her fingers together and watched intently.

"I hope she pulls it off!" Lou Lou said. She and Pea were both nervous for Abuela Josie since it had been so long since she'd done her one-foot-drag, around-the-world combo.

"I'm so happy she has her lucky hat to help her," replied Pea.

Everyone held their breath as Abuela Josie prepared for her stunt. She swung quickly from the saddle into the one-foot-drag. But before she did the around-the-world part, she reached into a saddlebag and pulled out her new red hat. Abuela Josie tossed her lucky hat at Pea, who caught it with ease, then Abuela Josie put her red one on for the second part of the stunt. She performed the rest perfectly, even managing to add in the belly flip.

"Bravo! Bravo!" shouted the crowd when she was done. Lou Lou and Pea cheered and whistled.

"I guess her new stunt is a one-foot-drag, *hat switch*, around-the-world, belly-flip combo," Lou Lou said, and Pea smiled.

Performance after performance followed. There was the Sugar Mountain Sisters' Shimmy danced by Danielle Desserts, her snooty-girl posse, and four Verde Valley girls, all wearing head-to-toe pink. Lou Lou wasn't a fan of the Sugar Mountain Sisters, but she had to admit the dance was pretty good. Pea's cousin Magdalena and her friends did a hula-hoop routine, high school choruses accompanied by their marching bands sang a song called "Todos Somos Amigos," and kinder-gartners handed out paper flowers and tamarindo candy, Lou Lou and Pea's favorite. Danny from La Frutería juggled mangoes, and Lou Lou's dad did a nautical-knot-tying demonstration. String quartets from two different neighborhoods performed a Bicentennial piece together.

"Do two quartets equal an eightet?" Lou Lou asked.

"I think it's an octet," replied Pea.

Kyle and Tommy weren't able to get their space goats to follow instructions, but they earned plenty of laughs when Jupiter ate his own helmet, as well as Mars Rover's, Mercury's, and Pluto's.

During a break before the closing ceremony, Lou Lou and Pea found Jeremy who was busy handing out fresh, delicious killer caracoles to the crowd. A cardboard crown with fake plastic jewels was perched on his red spiky head. On the front, in marker, were the words *Killer Caracoles King*.

"I suppose you expect us to call you Royal Highness," Lou Lou said.

"Naw," replied Jeremy. "Your Majesty will do just fine." Lou Lou and Pea laughed. "You're just in time. I have two caracoles left," Jeremy said. "I'm running out because they've been so popular. Monsieur Bonsoir from Verde Valley Bistro even asked if I'd consider an internship as a pastry chef this summer!"

"That's great!" Pea said.

Lou Lou broke one of the caracoles in half. "We can split this one and leave the other for someone else. Tonight is all about sharing, after all!"

Pea smiled. "Estoy orgullosa de ti," she said. Lou Lou gave Pea a blank stare. "I'm proud of you," Pea translated. "For being so thoughtful," she added. Lou Lou grinned.

A drumroll sounded the time for the closing ceremony. Lou Lou and Pea joined their families to watch. Pea straightened Blue Beauty on her head, and Lou Lou did the same with Pride of Pinky.

The crowd grew quiet as Mayor Montoya took the stage. It was twilight now, and the park was lit with the glowing Celebrar candles.

"¡Gracias a todos por venir a celebrar nuestro Bonanza de Bicentenario! Thank you, everyone, for coming to celebrate our Bicentennial Bonanza!" the mayor said. The crowd in La Fuente Park clapped. "And thank you also to the organizers and hosts from both El Corazón and Verde Valley," Mayor Montoya added to the sound of more enthusiastic clapping.

Lou Lou saw the Sammy's Gazebo Delivery truck waiting near the far side of the park and she hit her forehead with her palm.

"The gazebo, Pea!" she said. "Where will it go? In La Fuente Park or in Limonero Park? In Verde Valley or El Corazón?" Lou Lou had been so caught up in the day's events that she'd completely forgotten to consider

KILLER CARACOLES KING

which neighborhood would get the gazebo. But one thing was certain, it definitely wasn't going in the Argyles' backyard.

"I don't know—" Pea started.

"El Corazón has to get it back," replied Lou Lou. "It's only fair!"

"If we're getting it back, why is Sammy here in Verde Valley?" Pea asked. The mayor glanced at the truck and leaned toward the microphone. "I think we're about to find out." Pea answered her own question.

"There have been so many wonderful things about this day," Mayor Montoya said. "The delicious caracoles, the lovely honeysuckle, the amazing performances, the beautiful hats." Pea looked thrilled at the compliment.

"But the best thing of all," Mayor Montoya continued, "has been the display of friendship among all the neighborhoods in our city. Because of this, we will not be going forward with the gazebo as previously planned."

The crowd went silent and Lou Lou's heart sank. No gazebo for PSPP tea, kazoo concerts, and ice cream eating?

But Mayor Montoya wasn't finished. "Instead, we will put gazebos in both Limonero Park and La Fuente Park, as well as in every other neighborhood in our city!"

Lou Lou could hardly believe her ears. Everyone was getting a gazebo! The crowd's hush changed to a roar and Lou Lou and Pea jumped up and down, nearly losing their hats. They hugged their parents and Abuela Josie, and before they knew it, Jeremy and Rosa were there to celebrate along with them. Sarah unfurled the THANK YOU FOR THE GAZEBO!/¡GRACIAS POR EL MIRADOR! banners, Kyle's space goats ran in excited circles around the crowd, and Mr. Vila joined the happy fray.

"This news is great great!" he yelled.

From the stage, Mayor Montoya cried, *"Let's hold up our hats and say cheers to the past two hundred years!"*

"Cheers!" cried everyone, taking off their hats and waving them in the air.

"This has to be the best Bicentennial Bonanza ever," Pea said, and Lou Lou couldn't agree more.

CHAPTER TWENTY-NINE
PSPP

It was Friday afternoon and Lou Lou and Pea were exactly where they wanted to be—enjoying PSPP honeysuckle tea and caracoles in the gazebo in Limonero
Park. Lou Lou took a sip from her teacup and looked
around appreciatively.

"It really is very beautiful," she said of the ornate
wooden gazebo covered in colorful paintings of shapes,
flowers, and animals. "Wouldn't you agree, my dear?"
Lou Lou added politely.

Pea reached out to adjust Lou Lou's hat before putting
on her own. Wearing hats was Lou Lou and Pea's new

favorite PSPP tradition, and Pea was constantly crafting designs. When she was satisfied that the hats were perched at the correct angles, Pea leaned back and took a little bite of her caracol. She chewed slowly, with her mouth closed.

"Yes, it's lovely," said Pea. She ran her fingers over a golden plaque on the gazebo that read:

BICENTENNIAL BIRTHDAY
BONANZA GAZEBO
Dedicated to Peacock Pearl, Lou Lou Bombay,
Jeremy Ruiz & Comet Cop Kyle Longfellow

"I still can't believe the mayor dedicated it to us."

"I know! So amazing!" Lou Lou thought back to Mayor Montoya's announcement after the Bonanza that the Limonero Park gazebo would be dedicated to Lou Lou and Pea. Pea had insisted that Jeremy and Kyle also be included, though she'd avoided mentioning their role in the Diary Mission just in case it caused trouble for Kyle.

"So Ranchero Park in Centro Circle this weekend?" Pea asked.

"Definitely," Lou Lou replied. "That's the last one on

our list." Lou Lou and Pea had another new tradition. Every Sunday, their parents drove them to one of the gazebos in a different neighborhood in the city. Sometimes they brought lunch, sometimes Jeremy and Kyle tagged along, and there were always caracoles. Jeremy's killer caracoles were in serious demand these days, but he always had a few extras for Lou Lou and Pea.

Lou Lou and Pea sipped their tea in silence, lost in their thoughts. Lou Lou gazed at her honeysuckle and remembered the days leading up to the Bonanza. It had been a rocky road, but everything turned out wonderfully at the end. At least for everyone but the Argyles. Lou Lou and Pea hadn't seen Andy or Amanda since that day. Lou Lou wondered what had happened to them. Despite all the Argyles' devious deeds, she hoped they were okay. Lost in her thoughts, Lou Lou almost didn't hear the voice coming from the gazebo's arched opening.

"Um, excuse me." A face peered in at Lou Lou and Pea. Lou Lou sprang to her feet, overturning her cup and feeling heat rise in her ears. Pea's blue eyes went wide and she nearly dropped her caracol. It was none other than Amanda Argyle. Her hair was in long braids as always, and she was wearing an orange-and-red matching skirt and vest in her usual diamond print. But something was different—her *excuse me* didn't sound sarcastic or mean.

"May we help you?" Pea asked nicely but with a touch of caution in her voice.

"Actually, you can." Amanda stepped into the gazebo. She was holding a large bag, but Lou Lou couldn't see what was inside. Amanda wasn't smirking and she didn't look smug. Instead, she seemed a bit nervous.

"*How* exactly can we help you?" Lou Lou asked less politely than Pea. She righted her teacup.

"I was hoping you would let me apologize," Amanda said. This time, Pea was surprised enough to actually drop her caracol, and Lou Lou knocked over her cup again.

"Apologize?" Lou Lou asked, not quite believing her red ears.

"Yes." Amanda looked at her feet, then back up at Lou Lou and Pea. "I know what my dad and I did was wrong. You were right when you said that I don't have any friends. I felt sad and jealous every time I saw best friends like you two and, well, I guess it made me act mean."

"That's for sure," Lou Lou said. Pea nudged her gently. "I'm sorry. Go on."

"After the truth came out at the caracoles contest,

I hid across the street from La Fuente Park to watch the Bonanza. I saw how all the people from different neighborhoods were able to become friends and work together. I want to make new friends, too, ones who will laugh at my jokes, bring balloons to my birthday parties, and go with me to Cupcake Cabana on Saturdays."

Pea looked at Lou Lou and raised her eyebrows. Lou Lou sighed, but then nodded and smiled.

"Amanda, we accept your apology," Pea said. "Would you like to sit with us and have a caracol?"

Amanda brightened. "I'd love to!" Her eyes lit up. "But I can't stay long. Maybe just a quick bite or two?" Amanda sat down on the bench that ringed the inside of the gazebo and Pea handed her a pastry. "This is yummy," she said as she nibbled on the end.

"Jeremy made them," said Lou Lou.

"Can you please tell him that I'm sorry, too?" Amanda asked.

"Of course," answered Pea.

Amanda finished her caracol and licked the crumbs off her lips. "Before I go home, I wanted to give you this." Amanda took a pale blue box out of her bag. Lou Lou recognized it right away. It was Pea's hatbox, and inside was Pea's original blue hat that Amanda had snatched at the Heliotrope. She gave Pea the hat, and Pea turned it around in her hands. The bow was a little squished, but otherwise it was fine.

"I thought that having pretty hats might make people like me, but I see now that's not true. I should never have taken it from you," Amanda said.

"I'd like you to keep it," Pea said, much to Lou Lou's surprise. She handed the hat back to Amanda, whose jaw dropped. "It looks good on you," Pea added. "It still needs a name, though. How about Amigas de Amanda? Then, whenever you wear it, you'll be reminded of the two new friends you just made."

"I . . . I don't know what to say," Amanda replied. "Thank you! See you soon, I hope?"

"¡Hasta pronto!" said Pea. "Please do join us for PSPP again."

"I'll bring *three* teacups next time," added Lou Lou.

"I would love that," said Amanda. "And maybe I can take you up on your offer to go to Cupcake Cabana with me. My treat." She smiled, put Amigas de Amanda on her head, and bounded down the gazebo steps.

Lou Lou turned to Pea. "Wow, that was unexpected!" Pea nodded. "You were so kind to her, Pea. It was really amazing," Lou Lou said.

"Being kind is always in style," Pea replied with one of her fashion quotes.

"Who said that?" Lou Lou asked.

"Peacock Pearl, of course." Pea winked one bright blue eye.

PEA'S
Perfectly Marvelous Paper Hats

·>> MATERIALS <<·

- Paper bowls
- Paper plates (Pea had to clean caracol crumbs off Lou Lou's plate before starting.)
- Scissors (Be sure to have an adult help you when cutting materials for your hat!)
- Watercolors or other non-toxic craft paints
- Glue
- Ribbon, at least ½ inch wide and about 24 inches long (Pea chose blue for herself and a floral pattern for Lou Lou, but you should use your favorite pattern or color!)
- Optional decorations, like feathers, sequins, glitter, buttons, dried flowers, stamps, and so on!

·>> INSTRUCTIONS <<·

1. Turn your paper bowl upside down. Paint the bottom of the bowl with the colors of your choice. Set

the bowl aside to dry. (This will become the crown of your hat.)

2. Next, use your scissors to cut the center out of your paper plate to make a ring of the plate's edge approximately 1½ to 2 inches wide. (This will become the brim of your hat.) Later, you will place this ring over the upside-down bowl, so be sure the hole you've cut out is big enough to fit over the bowl, but not so big that the bowl falls through it. **And don't forget to have an adult help you use the scissors.**

3. Paint both sides of the paper plate ring with the same colors you used for your bowl—or with different colors, if you're feeling fashionably daring! Pea loves mixing and matching. Set the ring aside to dry.

4. When both your bowl and plate ring are dry, it's time to assemble your hat! Start by propping your bowl up, either by placing crumpled newspaper under it or by putting it atop a stack of other bowls.

5. Next, spread glue around the rim of your upside-down bowl.

6. Then lower the painted plate ring over the bowl and gently press down to help the glue seal it all

the way around. You've just attached the brim to the crown of your hat. Enjoy a snack while it dries!

7. Finally, it's time to decorate. First, glue your ribbon around the base of your crown to cover the seam between the crown and the brim of your hat. You can tie a bow in the back with any extra ribbon.

8. Add other design elements you might want, such as feathers (for Pea), sequins (for Ella Divine), or dried flowers (for Lou Lou). Set your perfectly marvelous hat aside one last time to dry.

Now it's fashion-show time! Wear your hat for PSPP or on a sunny stroll in the park with friends.

LOU LOU & PEA'S
Words to Know in Spanish

Note: Nouns in Spanish carry genders. Sometimes, one noun has two different genders to reflect the subject in question. If the suffix is an *a*, then it's a female noun. If it's an *o*, then it's a male noun.

abuela – grandmother

adiós – goodbye

almuerzo – lunch

amiga / amigo – female friend / male friend

   mi amiga / mi amigo – my friend

año(s) – year(s)

artista – artist or performer

azucar – sugar

bien / buena / bueno – well or good

bienvenidas – welcome

bisabuela – great-grandmother

bonita – beautiful

buenas noches – good evening or good night

buenas tardes – good afternoon

calaveras – sugar skulls

camelia – camellia

cena – dinner

chicas / chicos – girls / boys

claro – of course

cómo estás (tú) / cómo está (usted)?
    – how are you?

de nada – you're welcome

desayuno – breakfast

fácil – easy

flor(es) – flower(s)

gata / gato – cat

gracias – thank you

harina – flour

hasta luego – see you later!

hola – hello

hoy – today

huevos – eggs

ingrediente – ingredient

intuición – intuition

lista / listo – ready

lo siento – I'm sorry

luz – light

mamá – mother

mañana – tomorrow

mantequilla – butter

maravillosa / maravilloso – marvelous

mascota – pet

mejor – better

mija / mijo – my dear, or my child

mucha(s) / mucho(s) – many, a lot

muy bien – very good

niñas / niños – girls / boys

nosotros – we

noticias – news

orgullosa / orgulloso – proud

panadera / panadero – baker

papá – father

pasteles – pastries

perdón – excuse me

pero – but, however

perra / perro – dog

pobrecita / pobrecito – poor thing

por favor – please

preciosa / precioso – precious

prima / primo – cousin

problema – problem

quinceañera – fifteenth-birthday party

señora / señorita / señor – woman / young
woman / man

sí / no – yes / no

suerte – luck

taqueria – taco shop

teléfono – telephone

tengo – I have

tía / tío – aunt / uncle

tiempo – time

tú – you, informal (friends and siblings)

último – last

usted / ustedes – you, formal (parents and
    adults, singular) / you, formal (parents
    and adults, plural)

verdad – truth

yo – I